Knights Crossing

Jess Mowry

To Veronica

Knights Crossing

"All aboard!"

The conductor's voice sounded muffled, as if he was calling through layers of cotton instead of the hot steamy air. The engine hooted its whistle twice, then began puffing slowly away as if weary of working so hard in this heat but trapped on its tracks with no way to escape.

Skyler remained on the station platform, his new carpet bag at his feet, and watched the train vanish in vine-tangled trees, its clatter and chuffing fading away, leaving only wood smoke and sweltering silence in memory of its five-minute stop. He'd almost forgotten this heavy wet heat after spending a year in New Orleans, where he'd celebrated his thirteenth birthday only a few weeks ago. His white linen shirt clung sodden and tight to the softly aggressive orbs of his chest, while sweat trickled down the sides of his face from under his blond shoulder-length hair. Nothing moved in this sultry scene, where even the trees seemed to droop in exhaustion beneath their long burdens of gray Spanish moss.

In fact it was almost eerily still, like the ominous feeling in hurricane season just before a savage storm.

Skyler sucked air as thick as molasses that almost took conscious effort to breathe, wiped sweat from his forehead and looked around. An old man dozed on a wooden bench, a battered slouch hat pulled over his face... the same old man who'd been dozing there when Skyler had left a year ago. An equally ancient and dusty brown dog lay limply asleep at the man's booted feet -- probably also the very same dog -- and a pair of black boys were sprawled in the shade beneath a mossy water tank across the tracks from the station. A telegraph chattered inside the office, making a drowsy insect sound.

Skyler struggled to pull out his watch, which wasn't easy to do anymore because his belly had prospered this year and far overhung his brown canvas trousers... he'd left all his suits in New Orleans because they were now too small. These soft lolling pounds of pale opulence couldn't be contained by his shirt, and the funnel-shaped cave of his navel was peeking where a button had been. Skyler had always been chubby, but his aunt in 'Orleans owned an excellent cook and Skyler had been an appreciative patron of all her culinary arts.

He finally extracted his watch, nickel-plated and heavy, made for a boy's rough-and-tumble life, and a parting gift from his father last year... a reminder that "gentlemen were punctual." Flipping open its sturdy cover, he saw it was 12:46. The train had arrived on time, yet there was no one but the dozing old man, the slumbering dog and the lazy black boys. No buggy stood waiting to take him home.

"Well, damn!" he muttered, wiping more sweat from a chipmunk-cheeked face that boasted a small second chin. He supposed he shouldn't have been surprised; it was just like old Jupiter to fall asleep at the reins, and his horse would have sensibly stopped in shade. Although it was 1860, nothing seemed to have changed in this place, and probably never would.

The little town of Knight's Crossing, a dozen buildings surrounded by forest, was only a few minutes walk from the station, but Skyler didn't feel like walking, especially toting his heavy bag. He supposed he could sit by the man on the bench, or go inside the waiting room, where at least it was shady if not any cooler, but he wanted something to eat.

He stuffed the watch back in his pocket and glanced at the bucket and dipper that hung by the waiting room door, but the trickling leaks from the water tank would probably taste a lot better. What would *really* taste good was a big mug of beer from the cellar at home.

Where the devil was Jupiter?

The two black boys had noticed him. They seemed to be around his age, but both were shirtless, barefoot and dusty. One wore only the tatters of trousers, though the other boy's were in much better shape. The boy in rags was beautifully muscled and rather handsomely dark chocolate-brown. His chest jutted out like a small pair of bricks and his biceps looked like river rocks even while resting relaxed.

The other boy was as black as coal and the fattest boy of any color that Skyler had ever seen! His canvas trousers -- similar to Skyler's but three times the size -- were strained to the point of bursting their seams on legs that looked like oak tree trunks, while his belly both filled and spilled over his lap in an avalanche of ebony blubber. His chest was a pair of enormous black melons that made Skyler think of a mammy, and his mammoth body displayed more rolls than one might find in a French bakery. He was surely an astonishing sight, and Skyler found himself wondering how a slave boy could have had gotten so fat.

The muscular youth sprang to his feet and trotted up to Skyler, bringing a strong scent of earthy boy-sweat, which, except for his own, Skyler hadn't smelled in a year. "Carry your bag, suh?" he asked.

Skyler considered the offer, which he could have made a command: there was no way of knowing when Jupiter would get here. The town had a reasonably decent tavern that featured an ample free lunch, and Jupiter would guess he'd gone there. But, Skyler shook his head.

"No thanks," he said, though not sure why. He automatically dug in a pocket -- again with a struggle -- and handed the boy a penny to reward his subservience. Then he picked up his bag and crossed the tracks, his belly lolling with every step while the orbs of his chest jiggled and bobbed, and feeling new sweat soaking his shirt from the effort it took to move in this heat. He stopped in front of the huge fat boy, who looked up from under a wild bush of hair, his eyes as black as polished onyx and the hint of a smile on his full pouty lips. His behind was so big and his trousers half off so he really sat *on* them instead of in them.

3

"Boy," said Skyler. "Y'all want to carry my bag to town?"

The enormous boy only widened his smile, a lazy, slow, and foxy expression. "I'd really rather not."

Skyler felt his cheeks flush pink. He couldn't believe what he'd heard! There were many freed slaves in New Orleans, while mulatto children were always free no matter how dark they were; and Skyler had learned to be tolerant when Negroes addressed him as if they were equals -- *gentlemanly* Negroes, of course, which had first seemed a contradiction of terms -- but that had been in a modern city where one had to make allowances for changing times and new ideas, not right here in his own home town!

Skyler fought to control his anger, which made him sweat all the more. "That wasn't a question, boy," he said in a warning tone.

The gargantuan youth only heaved a huge sigh. "I s'pose not." He then took a minute to yawn and stretch, all his rolls rearranging themselves with every leisurely movement. "How much you pay me, young massa?"

"I *might* give you a penny... if you don't give me any more sass."

The boy raised a soot-colored eyebrow. "Sorry, young suh. I just couldn't do it for less than a nickel." Then he grinned with startling teeth, like the oversize chompers of some mighty beast. "Why, other niggers would talk!"

Skyler's cheeks flashed like a railroad warning. "Who you belong to, boy?" he demanded.

The mammoth boy looked oddly amused. "Massa Franklin at Content."

"Then why aren't you out there working?" snapped Skyler.

"Massa Franklin give me this day, an' a nickel to buy me some candy... suh. Both of which I have been enjoyin'."

Skyler glanced toward the town, hoping to see the dust of a buggy rising above the treetops, but nothing moved in the hellish heat. The muscular boy had followed him and was standing submissively near.

"I carries your bag for that penny, suh." He patted his paving stone chest seemingly not showing off but merely illustrating a fact. "I's fairly strong."

"Then why aren't *you* working?" growled Skyler.

"I's been sold to a white boy, suh. I's gonna be his 'panion, I's told... tho' I don't rightly know what that mean. But they sent me here a day early, an' I don't have the slightest of money."

Skyler frowned. "*Who* you say you been sold to, boy?"

"I means a young massa, suh."

"That's better," said Skyler. "I assume you have papers to prove what you say?"

"Sho' does, suh. Right here in my pocket, 'long with my bill of sale."

"I don't need to see them," said Skyler. "Y'all don't look like a fool, so I know you wouldn't be lyin' to me."

He studied the boy for a moment; a very sturdily-built buck an inch or two taller than himself with somewhat startling bright amber eyes and a cheerful, rather intelligent face with a wide snubby nose, and expressive full lips. He didn't have a lot of mass, but every young muscle was starkly defined like an artist's anatomy model. His trousers -- what remained of them -- barely clung to his narrow hips, revealing a few sooty curls. He was also more than a little smelly, though Skyler wasn't bothered by that, having grown up playing with slaves; and he probably smelled a little himself from sweating for hours on the train.

Skyler had never had a companion, at least not a boy of his very own, but some young master was fortunate to be getting such a handsome gift.

"I don't want your help," said Skyler. That sounded ungentle-manly so he added, "But, thanks all the same. ...I hope you like your new master." That wasn't a proper thing to say: of course it was good if a slave liked his master, but what really mattered was they obeyed.

He struggled to dig in his pocket again. "Here's a dime for some-thing to eat." He glanced at the sky overhead, as empty and blue as a porcelain bowl, though growing darker off to the south. "Y'all best find you a dry place to sleep 'cause it look like to storm before evenin'." He considered, then added: "Go see the blacksmith in town, Jethro Hill. Tell him Skyler Knight sent you. I 'spect he'll let you sleep in his shop."

"Thank you, suh!" said the boy with a smile, flashing white teeth as bright as his eyes and taking the dime like a diamond. "But, don't y'all want me to carry your bag?"

"No," said Skyler, though again not sure why. This boy could have probably carried *him* along with his bulky baggage. "Y'all best be goin'," he added. "Folks 'round here don't like seein' niggers with nothin' constructive to do. An' I don't advise bein' out after dark."

"Thank you, suh," the boy said again, then trotted obediently off toward town.

"That was very kind of you, suh," the huge fat boy remarked.

Skyler shrugged. "I didn't want him gettin' in trouble." He realized he'd been dropping his "G's" despite a year of refinement in school, and dropped his bag on the ground. "All right, I'll pay you a nickel. But, you're trying my patience, boy."

"You just gave him a dime for nothin'."

"Shut up an' get up!" roared Skyler. "Or I'll give *you* somethin' you won't soon forget!"

The fat boy only smiled again and struggled to get to his feet. After several half-hearted tries, he gasped, "Can you give me a hand, young massa? I's too fat to get up by myself."

"Well, damn!" Skyler grabbed the huge boy's hand, which featured dimples instead of knuckles, but that accomplished nothing except making him sweat all the more. Finally, he knelt and shoved a shoulder beneath an enormous blubber-bulked arm. After several minutes of struggle he managed to get the boy on his feet.

The fat boy's trousers almost fell off, but he reached down over the rolls of his sides and tugged them halfway up his bottom, which looked like two ebony planets colliding. He wasn't any taller than Skyler, but seemed at least four times as wide, especially around the middle. His trouser cuffs puddled over his feet, and his wobbly mass of belly blubber hung all the way to his knees in a pair of pendulous teardrop shapes, while his navel resembled a railroad tunnel vanishing into blackness between them.

"Let's go," said Skyler, whose shirt was now sullied with muddy dust and even more soaked with the fat boy's sweat, making Skyler his aromatic twin. "What's your name?"

6

"Loki, suh, but I goes by Lucky."

"Well, hurry up, Lucky, I don't have all day."

But, Lucky didn't hurry. It seemed to take every ounce of his strength just to pick up Skyler's bag, and he waddled along at the pace of a snail, his huge belly rolling against his vast thighs, his body rippling and quaking all over, every inch of him in motion, while he dragged the bag behind in the dust instead of properly carrying it. His thighs seemed to get in each other's way, making each step a major event, and he dropped the bag about every ten feet to tug up his trousers again. Skyler had to wait when this happened, and was getting hotter and angrier with every passing minute.

Lucky was puffing like a locomotive by the time they were half-way to town. He dropped Skyler's bag in the dirt once more as his trousers slid down to his ankles, and wiped gleaming sweat from his triple-chinned face. "I's sorry, young massa," he wheezed as if dying. "I's just too fat for this kind of work."

"Damn you, boy!" bellowed Skyler. "Pick up that bag and come on!"

"I can't, suh," Lucky panted. "An' I can't reach my trousers."

Skyler muttered another curse, tugged Lucky's trousers halfway up his bottom, then snatched the bag himself. He turned to stalk away, but then hesitated and turned back around. "Come on, boy! At least you can watch my bag for me. You're not too fat for that, are you?"

"Sho', young massa, I watch real good. But I wants me another nickel."

"What!" cried Skyler. "You haven't earned your first nickel! I wouldn't give you a tin picayune for all you've done so far!"

"But I tried to please you, massa. Ain't that my purpose in life?"

"You're *not* pleasin' me!" Skyler almost howled. "What do you do out at Franklin's?"

"I thinks a lot, suh. An' I tell my thinkin's to Massa Franklin, who sets a great store by 'em, suh."

"Don't mess with me, boy!" Skyler yelled. "Nobody owns a thinkin' nigger!"

The fat boy only smiled again. "Y'all might be right about that.

But I helps my mammy in the cook house... when I ain't doin' my thinkin'. She be the best cook in the world."

"As if you knew anything about the world!" Skyler poked Lucky's gigantic belly, his finger sinking half out of sight. "It's obvious you work around food. Likely as not you steal it, too."

"Oh no, suh! I whistle all the way up the walk."

"Don't lie to me, boy! Ain't no way an honest nigger could get as fat as you!"

Lucky patted Skyler's belly as if he was fluffing a pillow. "But honest white folks can?"

"I'm a human being!" snapped Skyler. "You're just an intelligent animal."

"What's the difference, suh?"

"The difference is somebody owns you. Now, come on, God-dammit!"

"What about my nickel, suh?"

"Here!" yelled Skyler, digging with effort into a pocket and hurling a coin at the smiling boy, who caught it easily. "Now, COME ON!"

Skyler was puffing himself by the time they reached the tavern with Lucky waddling slowly behind and every step like an earthquake in pudding. Though purportedly too fat to carry Skyler's bag, he seemed to have plenty of breath to whistle a cheerful tune as he walked.

The tavern was brick with a roofed veranda. The scents of food and fresh foamy beer drifted out through its open front doors. Skyler paused at the steps to study the sky.

"I feels it, too," said Lucky. "There be a big storm comin' on."

"Animals can always sense trouble," Skyler muttered sarcastically. He mounted the steps and dropped his bag. There were tables and chairs on the pouch, but it would be cooler inside. "Here, boy," he said. "Sit yourself down an' watch my bag."

"Could you give me a hand up the steps, suh?"

Sweating more than ever, Skyler helped Lucky ascend. "Good God, boy, don't sit in a *chair!*"

Lucky smiled. "You're perfectly right, I'd bust it, suh." He plopped down on the boards of the porch and the whole building seemed to shake. "I guards your bag with my life."

"You damn well better, it's worth a lot more!" Skyler hoisted his slipping trousers and started to enter the doorway, but Lucky gave him a wistful look.

"I sho' is hungry, young suh. An' awful thirsty, too."

Skyler sighed. "I'll bring you somethin'... something."

Chapter Two

The tavern's interior was relatively cool. A gallery encircled its second floor where rooms could be rented for the night... also by the hour. The windows were thickly begrimed so most of the light came through the doorway. A long oak bar with a tarnished brass rail filled one side of the room, with a mirror, and bottles on shelves behind it. Tables and chairs were scattered around, including a big one that held the free lunch. A couple of loungers stood at the bar, their tattered clothes and grimy slouch hats revealing them as share-croppers. One of them had a small bull-whip coiled and tied to his belt, proof that he was wealthy enough to afford at least one slave. Some better-dressed men occupied a few tables, and there was a card game in progress. The air was hazed with cigar smoke, which blended well with the scents of food and malty aroma of beer. Skyler adjusted his trousers again: he supposed he should have bought a new pair, but much of the money his father sent had been spent dining out in New Orleans.

The tavern-keeper was a brown-bearded, beer-bellied, ruddy-faced man who smiled as Skyler strode up to the bar. "Afternoon, suh," he said, then added, "Why, you're Skyler Knight."

"Afternoon, Tom," replied Skyler.

"Ain't seen you around in seem like a year. Where y'all been keepin' yourself?"

Skyler briefly related his past year in New Orleans, then ordered a beer. He put a nickel on the bar, but the tavern-keeper smiled again. "It's on me, suh. Welcome home."

"Thank you, Tom," said Skyler, and raised the foaming mug in salute. "Your health, suh." He went to the table to build a sandwich, but noticed Lucky peeping in. The tavern-keeper had noticed him, too, and the poor white men were scowling.

"That your boy?" asked Tom. "If he ain't, I'll run him off."

"He's watching my bag," said Skyler, imagining Lucky trying to run, which made a funny picture. "Another beer, if you please."

"Y'all buy him down in 'Orleans, suh?" asked the tattered man with the whip.

Skyler almost said no. Many young gentlemen had companions, who also functioned as personal servants. In England they were called squires; and he'd read a lot about knights in the ancient days of chivalry. "He's watching my bag," Skyler repeated, speaking the truth while implying a lie.

"He'll have to go around back," said Tom. "Sorry, suh."

"Of course," agreed Skyler. He paid his nickel, then took the second mug out to Lucky. The other poor white regarded his mug and muttered something about sanitation, but the tavern-keeper told him to hush.

Lucky gulped down half the beer as soon as Skyler gave it to him. "Mmmm!" he panted, finally coming up for air. "That sho' is good, young massa! But, you ain't forgot my lunch, has you?"

"No I ain't... haven't," said Skyler. "But you have to go around back."

"S'pect it be cooler back there." Lucky got to his feet with surprising ease. "Bring your bag, suh, so I can keep watchin'." He waddled away with the mug in hand while Skyler followed toting the bag. The rear of the tavern was shaded by trees and was cooler than the front. Lucky sprawled with his back to the bricks and gulped down the rest of his beer. "I could use me another one, suh. An' I sho' is powerful hungry."

"All right!" cried Skyler, flinging his bag beside the huge boy and raising a puff of dust. "I haven't tasted my own, thanks to you!"

"But I's guardin' your property, suh."

"I could have taken it inside."

"You could have carried it yourself."

"...Are you givin' me sass again?"

"No, young massa, just thinkin' is all."

"Well, don't, it'll get you in trouble."

"I was thinkin' about my other nickel."

"Here, dammit!" Going in through the tavern's back door, Skyler took a gulp from his mug, then went to the table and grabbed a plate. There was roast beef, ham, and loaves of bread, pickles, onions, salted potatoes and hard-boiled eggs, among many other tempting things. Skyler constructed a big beef sandwich... then a new thought came to his mind. He knew Lucky was teasing him... the boy seemed not only surprisingly smart but endowed with a daring sense of humor. Skyler wasn't sure why he'd chosen Lucky instead of the muscular buck to serve him. Maybe he'd been curious about a boy so fat? No one knew much about Franklin's plantation. A few slave owners raised "oddities" to be sold to traveling shows, and Lucky was certainly odd. Or, maybe he was a pet and only kept to amuse his master like jesters in the days of yore? That would account for his sassiness, being allowed to become so fat, and dammable lack of respect. Then, Skyler started to pile the plate with everything in sight. He added so much that the tavern-keeper raised a critical eyebrow.

"Beggin' your pardon, Master Knight, but y'all could put me out of business."

"I'll pay for this, Tom," said Skyler. "And another beer, if you please."

One of the gamblers looked up from his cards. "If I may be allowed an observation, you can't possibly eat all that, suh."

"It's not for me," said Skyler. "That boy... of mine... is uppity, an' I'm about to teach him a lesson."

The man cocked his head. "An' what might that be, if I may inquire?"

"He's been sassin' me like an infernal imp, an' now he's cryin' he's hungry. Well, if he can't eat what I give him, I believe I'll borrow that good man's whip and teach him a lesson in manners, suh."

The poor white man at the bar raised his mug. "I'll sho' nuff drink to that, suh!"

Everyone watched with interest as Skyler heaped more food on the plate. "Lord, Master Knight," said Tom. "Y'all gonna bust me!"

"I'm gonna bust somethin'," laughed Skyler.

"It's on me, Tom," said the gambler. Then he turned to Skyler. "Y'all be a bettin' man, suh?"

"Ever hear of The House of the Rising Sun?"

The man seemed impressed... though Skyler didn't say that he'd never been inside the place.

"Y'all cuttin' a prosperous figure, suh," the gambler went on. "An' no denying your boy is, so I guess y'all don't lose much. But I got me a shiny new double eagle says your boy can't eat all that."

"I'm in," said another gambler.

"Just sold a 'ninny yesterday," boasted the man with the whip, "so if you gentlemen would allow me...?"

"All right," agreed Skyler, finished at last and admiring the mountain of food he'd built. "Y'all want Tom to hold the bets?"

The gambler smiled. "I always trust a cherubic face... meanin' no offense, suh. But, that boy of yours is gonna be thirsty after eatin' all that beef an' ham an' salty boiled potatoes. I ought to buy him a couple more beers."

"All right," said Skyler. He studied the heaping plate, knowing, of course, he'd lose this bet... Lucky *couldn't* eat all that! But, sending Lucky waddling home with a couple of stripes across his bottom for being so dammably sassy was more than worth a few dollars.

Skyler enjoyed the look of dismay on the ebony moon of Lucky's face when he carried the plate out back, followed by Tom with three mugs of beer, the pair of gentleman gamblers, and the ragged man with the whip.

"Here, boy," said Skyler, shoving the plate into Lucky's hands. "If you can't eat that after troubling me, I'll be in my rights to give you a thrashing."

The poor white eagerly offered his whip. Skyler had never held one before -- his father's slaves seldom needed a lash -- but the supple leather felt good in his hands and gave him a feeling of power.

Lucky stared at the mountain of food. "Oh lord, young massa, I can't eat all this!"

Skyler curled the whip. "Eat it or else!"

"That's tellin' him, suh!" laughed the poor white man.

Lucky looked trapped for a moment, but then began to eat. Tom set down the trio of mugs.

"You said you were thirsty, too," Skyler added. "I hope for the sake of your bottom you are!"

Everyone watched in expectant silence as Lucky ate and drank. For a while there were only the sounds of chomping and guzzling gulps of beer. Somehow the vittles were vanishing! But then he began to slow down, forcing himself to chew and swallow. Still, he kept stuffing in food. The poor white looked uncertain, while the gambler cocked his head. Lucky was panting and pouring sweat, but had eaten two-thirds of the mountain of food, and only one mug of beer remained.

Skyler began to feel guilty... possibly even ashamed. This suddenly seemed rather crude, if not cruel. "That's enough," he finally said. "I think you've learned your lesson."

The gamblers chuckled and Tom looked relieved -- folks always said he had a good heart -- but the poor white muttered, "A bet's a bet, boy!"

"Mind who you're calling boy," said Skyler.

"Sorry, suh."

Lucky massaged his massive middle. "But I can't stop now, young massa, you lose all that money on me."

"It's not important," said Skyler.

The gambler slapped Skyler's back. "Your boy's got spirit, I'll give him that."

Skyler dropped the whip on the ground and knelt beside the panting Lucky. "I said you can stop."

"No, young massa," gasped Lucky. "You put your trust in me."

"It was only a joke... and in rather poor taste."

Lucky might have winked. "Don't taste bad at all, suh."

There were only two potatoes left, some slices of beef and the last mug of beer. Lucky managed to finish it all and blasted a thunderous burp.

The gambler laughed. "I'd never believed it if I hadn't seen it! If you wasn't an obvious gentleman, suh, I'd suspect I'd been taken in."

"He's a gentleman down to his bones," said Tom. "His family founded this town."

The poor white grumbled under his breath, but settled his loss and snatched up his whip. The gamblers paid off and went back in the tavern, and Lucky subsided against the wall.

"Are you all right?" asked Skyler, worried for Lucky now... and not about having to pay for him in case he was somehow damaged.

Lucky smiled, his eyes almost shut, his fingers clasped over his titanic belly as if to prevent an explosion. "I never hurt so good in my life."

Skyler touched Lucky's shoulder. "You sure you gonna be all right?"

"'Spect I just sleep for a while, suh. I generally does after lunch before supper."

The tavern-keeper returned. "Your buggy's out front, Master Knight."

"Thank you, Tom," said Skyler. Then he turned back to Lucky. "I'll give you a ride out to Franklin's. No denying you earned it. An' here's five dollars. That ought to keep you in candy awhile."

"Huh?" asked Lucky, nearly asleep.

Skyler shook the huge boy's shoulders, making him ripple all over. "Come on now, wake up. I said I'll give you a ride home."

"But I's too stuffed to move."

"I'll help you. Come on."

That wasn't easy. Lucky's vast body was slippery with sweat and it took several minutes of straining and struggle to finally get him on his feet. Skyler was panting and gasping himself, but he pulled Lucky's arm over his shoulders and helped him waddle away.

Chapter Three

Jupiter hadn't changed a bit, a wrinkled old raisin with snowy white wool who moved at the speed of an arthritic snail. Skyler had never been sure of Jupiter's purpose in life; he wasn't an actual house slave, though he came in the house whenever he pleased and even the butler was scared of him. And he didn't work in the fields, unless it was tending his own little garden. Nor was he trained at a trade, though he could do almost anything. He wasn't an overseer, but Skyler's father consulted him in matters concerning the slaves; and he always appeared to be busy with something, though only Skyler seemed to notice he actually did very little. Whatever he was supposed to do, he'd always had time to take Skyler fishing, or hunting or riding, or just tell him stories. He and his wife had their own little cabin between the Big House and the Quarters, and a lot of Skyler's childhood had been spent beneath its vine-covered roof. Jupiter had seen a lot in over seventy years on earth, but his eyebrows threatened to topple his hat when Skyler staggered around the tavern supporting the gigantic Lucky.

Jupiter composed and said, "Sorry I's late, Massa Knight, but I can't move as fast as I used to."

Skyler gave the old man a smile. "Meanin' you fell asleep on the road. Good to see you, Juppy. An' my name is still Skyler. ...Y'all know this boy?"

"I's seen him around now an' then, but we's never traded words. He belong to Franklin out at Content. ..."Scuse my ignorance, Sky, but what y'all doin' with him?"

Skyler laughed. "You've never been ignorant, Juppy. He had him a little too much for lunch. We'll take him to Franklin's before we go home."

Jupiter studied the heavens. "Your folks is gonna be worried, Sky. 'Specially with a storm comin' on, an' we's already late. Be 'least a hour out to Content."

Puffing hard, Skyler helped Lucky waddle around to the rear of the buggy. "I'll have Tom send someone home with a message. Let's get Lucky aboard."

That was easier said than done. It was four feet up to the buggy's bed, and Lucky was just about helpless. Jupiter was fairly strong, but Skyler had done very little this year but eat and leisurely stroll the city so his muscles had softened a lot. After what seemed like an hour of struggle they'd managed to get Lucky halfway in with much of his belly, bottom and legs still in unloaded limbo, but try as they might, grunting and gasping, they couldn't lift the rest of him. Skyler was ready to yell for Tom when the muscular buck from the station appeared.

"Y'all be needin' some help, suh?"

"Bless you, boy!" panted Skyler.

The young buck's muscles completed the task, and Lucky was finally rolled aboard, where he instantly went to sleep.

"Thanks," puffed Skyler, mopping more sweat from his face. The buttons had burst on his sodden shirt, and he peeled it off his glistening body, as "peaches-and-cream" as his cherubic face, his chest orbs adorned with pale pink nipples inverted like soft little slits. "You find the blacksmith?"

"Yes, suh." The boy glanced toward the southern sky. "It gonna be stormin' fit to bust 'fore the sun go down, but I gots me a roof to sleep under tonight."

"Go around back of the tavern," said Skyler. "I'll buy you a beer an' somethin' to eat an' Tom will bring it out." He dug in his pocket. "An' here's a dollar for your help."

"Lord!" exclaimed the boy. "I never had so much money a'fore! Now I see why they calls him Lucky!"

Skyler patted the boy's bushy head. "Your new master is lucky gettin' a good boy like you... but don't you tell him that."

17

Skyler accompanied the boy to get his bag from behind the tavern, then went inside to buy him a meal and have a message sent home. Finally, he returned to the buggy and climbed on the seat beside Jupiter. Jupiter flicked the reins and they rattled slowly out of town along a road that wound through the swamp, tunneling under cypress trees festooned with dangling streamers of moss. Skyler tossed his shirt in the back and stretched his sweat-sheened body, which jiggled about to the jolts of the buggy.

"It's good to be home an' free again. I hated all them fancy-ass clothes I had to wear in the city."

"Welcome home, Sky," said Jupiter. He grinned and poked Skyler's belly. "Y'all cuttin' a prosperous figure these days."

"You wouldn't believe the food in 'Orleans! It's positively meteoric!"

"Ain't hard to believe lookin' at you."

Then Skyler frowned. "But, dammit, I didn't have any lunch. An' I'm thirsty as hellfire."

"They's a water jug 'neath the seat. An' here, I brung your hat. ...'Less you wearin' one of them stovepipes now."

"You mean like Abraham Lincoln?" Skyler frowned again. "Those things look ridiculous! As ridiculous as some his notions."

"Don't know 'bout none of his notions, Sky, but I does agree 'bout them hats."

"You're better not knowin' about his notions, but thanks for bringin' my hat." Skyler clamped the old leather hat on his head. It was a boyish and savage adornment, boasting a rattlesnake skin for a band -- he'd shot and skinned the snake himself -- along with a jaunty hawk feather. "S'pect it be the only thing that fit me anymore at home. I surely missed my buckskin trousers."

Jupiter smiled. "I 'spect we can entice my missus into makin' y'all a new pair. 'Course, you be all growed up now, so some things gonna need changin'. Can't be lookin' like a injun-boy an' runnin' half bare in the swamp no more."

"If I have to change I'll change when *I'm* ready." Skyler pulled a crockery jug from underneath the seat and took several gulps of hot, flat water. "I really wanted a beer, dammit." He reached in his bag for a box of cigars. "I got these for you. Come clear from Cuba."

Jupiter took the box reverently, and Skyler took over the reins. "Hope you like 'em, Juppy."

"Lord, they look too fine to smoke!"

Skyler laughed. "That be their purpose in life. Y'all got a match, fulfill their purpose."

"I do believe I will." Jupiter pulled out a match box. "Care to join me, Sky?"

"Nah, Juppy, they all for you."

"Good things in life be better when shared."

"If you insist."

Skyler and Jupiter took cigars, and Jupiter struck a sulfur match on the buggy's iron brake lever. Then he recovered the reins, and Skyler sighed out smoke. "Reckon they had a fine big lunch waitin' for me at home."

Jupiter ducked a tendril of moss as they rattled under a low tree branch. "Well, yes an' no."

Skyler cocked his head. "What do you mean?"

Jupiter blew out smoke and frowned. "Your daddy had to sell Ruthie last month, an' the meals been shames to a sharecropper's table ever since she been gone. Your lunch be waitin' all right, but I wouldn't be callin' it fine by any stretch of that word."

"Huh?" said Skyler. "Why would he ever sell Ruthie?"

"'Cause he had to sell Ruthie's daughter, an' you know how he feel about bustin' up families. Your daddy always had him a heart when it come to things like that."

"You mean he sold Suzie, too?"

"Sho' nuff, Sky."

"But, she was only about my age."

Jupiter tapped the horse's rump with the buggy whip. "Damn little fool! Got herself in a family way with a field-buck over at Benson's place so your daddy sold her to Benson. An' natcherly Ruthie go with her."

"Why didn't father buy Benson's buck?"

"Wasn't good breedin' stock... not the sharpest knife in the drawer an' undersize for his age, though I guess his breedin' parts work good enough."

Skyler shook his head. "Benson sure got the best of that deal! Ruthie was a wonderful cook. So, who's cookin' now?"

"One of the young girls fresh out the Quarters... Betty her name. An' lord she could burn a potful of water!"

"Well, damn!" muttered Skyler. He glanced at the slumbering Lucky, watching him wobble, ripple and quake as the buggy bounced over ruts and holes. "He told me his mammy's a real good cook, which sure ain't hard to believe... boy must weigh at least four-hundred pounds."

Jupiter laughed. "Felt more like five to me, tryin' to get him off the ground."

"Hmmm," said Skyler, glancing at Lucky again.

Chapter Four

Seth Franklin's plantation was not very large. Nor was it known around Knight's Crossing for being especially prosperous, though Skyler had never met the man and didn't know much about him.

The drive to the Big House of vine-covered brick was bordered with rounded river rocks, though wasn't graveled to keep down the dust like the much grander entrance to Skyler's home. The welcoming archway out on the road was simply built of cedar logs with the name, CONTENT, carved into the cross-beam. The land was nearly surrounded by swamp, making it almost an island, and Franklin grew rice on his wetter grounds and sugar cane on the driest.

Lucky was still sleeping peacefully as they rolled up the drive between two fields where stalks of cane grew green and tall. The afternoon air was brutally hot, and the stormy feeling had increased. Skyler studied the sky to the south; its haze had taken a coppery tone, and he hoped he'd be home and eating supper before the fury broke.

There were only about twenty slaves at work -- men, women, and older youths -- out cutting cane in the steamy fields, and Skyler noted that, unlike some masters, Franklin didn't lock masks on his slaves to keep them from eating the cane. But maybe he didn't have to because they all looked very well-fed and, he supposed, as happy as could be expected of people who had to work in this heat. He saw three boys of around his own age, two in brown trousers like Lucky's, the third wearing only a loincloth -- an "African" garment most masters banned -- and all of them were chubby. One boy almost looked like himself... except for being a negro, of course. The men were heavy but handsomely built, and none of the women and girls were thin. Their pace as they worked was leisurely, and Skyler's father would have frowned.

The Big House looked impressive enough, two stories tall with a large portico, though less than half the size of Skyler's. The Quarters were out in plain sight behind it instead of being tastefully hidden and seemed to be in a lot better shape than dwellings of many poor whites. Flowers were growing around the cabins, and young children played on the Big House's lawn -- something else that most masters banned -- though some were old enough to be working.

"Ain't no wonder Franklin's not rich," Skyler remarked while donning his shirt. "He's let his slaves get fat an' lazy. ...An' look at those kids doin' nothin'!"

"Shameful, ain't it?" said Jupiter.

The children ran to the buggy as it came to a stop in front of the house... another liberty Skyler's father wouldn't have permitted. Like the older kids out in the fields, all were chubby or very well-fed, the males clad only in trousers, the females wearing simple shifts. One boy, in fact, who might have been twelve, was so enormous that Skyler stared. He wasn't *quite* as fat as Lucky if measured in actual pounds, but he seemed to be made of night-colored pudding instead of skin and bones. He waddled out from the shade of the house, leaning way back to balance a belly than cascaded nearly down to his knees. His breasts were as round as a full-figured girl's, and Skyler had to study his face to really be sure of his sex. He must have been the stable boy, as evidenced by a battered blue cap atop his woolly bush of hair. He was eating a chunk of cornbread and honey, and really needed three hands... one to hold the horse's collar, another to keep his trousers on, and a third to feed his triple-chinned face. The other kids spied Lucky asleep and started to giggle and laugh.

"Y'all figure out what to do with him," Skyler said to Jupiter. He adjusted his hat and climbed down from the buggy, automatically searching his pockets and passing out pennies to all the kids. "Mind that horse," he said to the blubbery stable boy while handing him a nickel. "She spooks like a colt when it thunders."

Something stirred the sultry air as Skyler approached the house: it was more like a warning than merely a breeze, and he glanced toward the southern sky again. There came a distant thunder crash like the boom of a faraway cannon, and the slaves in the fields stopped their work and began walking back to the Quarters. The house's front door swung gently open as Skyler mounted the steps to the porch. He tripped and almost fell in surprise... instead of a butler or maid, a chubby young ebony girl appeared.

She seemed to be around Skyler's age and was wearing only a simple slave dress, its blue cotton clinging so wonderfully tight that it clearly revealed every curve of her body... and there were an abundance of them. Her silky skin was as dark as jet, her face round-cheeked and button-nosed. Her hair was a halo of ringlets, and her eyes were large, silkily-lashed, and sparkled like polished obsidian.

Skyler regained his balance and pulled off his hat before realizing how absurd that was. He tried not to stare at the beautiful and wonderously voluptuous girl. Then, he felt himself blushing!

His voice sounded froggish, and he clutched his hat in nervous hands like a sharecropper begging a favor. "Um... is your mass..." He cleared his throat and began again in what he hoped was a manly tone. "Is your master at home?"

The girl smiled sweetly, dimpling her cheeks and flashing a crescent of snowy white teeth. Her eyes swept over Skyler and he could almost feel them like warm summer rain on his body. He fought to control his own eyes, wanting to look at this girl, knowing he had every right to look, but feeling stupidly shy. He realized she had spoken. "Huh?" he asked like an idiot.

"Who should I say is calling, please?" the girl repeated with the hint of a giggle.

"...Oh. My name is Skyler. ...Skyler Knight."

"Won't you step in, Master Knight?"

Still clutching his hat like a fool, Skyler came in as the girl moved aside. He didn't want her to curtsey for him, and thankfully she didn't. Her dress, he noted, was spotless, and her scent was some-how like water-lilies. She closed the door behind them after taking a look at the threatening sky.

"This way, please, Master Knight." She led him up a hallway, her bare feet soundless on polished oak. Skyler couldn't keep his eyes from watching her wonderfully rounded figure straining the indigo cloth. He got the impression that many paintings were hung along the walls, but he hardly noticed, whatever the art, being entranced by the girl, who ushered him into a library.

"Master Franklin is having a nap, but I'm sure he won't mind receiving you. I'll just be a minute, suh, please have a seat."

"Um," said Skyler, strangling his hat. It certainly wasn't proper, but he couldn't seem to help himself. "My name is Skyler. May I ask yours?"

The girl's eyes seemed to linger on him, and again he could almost feel them. "Lucinda."

Skyler swallowed. "That's a real pretty name."

"Thank you." Lucinda smiled and added, "Skyler. That's a very handsome name."

Skyler just stood with his hat in hands after Lucinda left the room. "Positively meteoric!" he murmured, then suddenly growled, "Don't be an ass! ...And, even if she wasn't a slave..."

He forced a scowl and closed his mouth before he said something else stupid, even if only to himself. He'd seen many girls in New Orleans, girls of his own... well, kind. So why was he behaving this way about a... Negro servant? Several of the children outside resembled African cupids, and he wondered if he'd been shot in the back with one of those mythical arrows.

He tried to shake off what felt like a spell -- though he wasn't sure what a spell would feel like -- and looked around the room. The furniture was all very old in a style now long out of fashion, but looked well cared-for and cherished. The air was pleasantly cool, the sunlight tamed by wine-colored drapes, but Skyler's shirt was thoroughly soaked, as well as begrimed from his struggles with Lucky. He probably smelled as sweaty and male as the young buck he'd met at the station. His boots were appallingly dusty, and his canvas trousers were really quite common. He hoped Franklin would not be displeased, though he worried more about the impression he might have made on Lucinda. ...And that was *really* absurd!

He forced his mind to other things; considered the chubby children again -- not to mention mammoth Lucky and the almost as blubbery stable boy -- and wondered, as he had at the tavern, if Franklin bred "oddities," perhaps to supplement whatever profits he made from his crops.

He became aware of more paintings around him, and though he knew very little of art, they all appeared to be skillfully done. Most were landscapes and bayou scenes, but others were slave children, usually chubby. There were scores of leather-bound books on the shelves, and Skyler began to study their titles. It seemed as if Franklin was very well-read: there were Shakespeare, Dante, Cervantes, Poe, Dickens, DeFoe and Hawthorne, plus volumes of Philosophy, as well as many religious tomes. There were also books about Africa; and Skyler was scanning their well-worn spines when Lucinda's soft voice surprised him. He turned around, feeling stupidly shy, like a poor white waiting to ask for a loan and ill at ease in a gentleman's house. Which, of course, was *completely* absurd! His own house was ten-times grander than Franklin's... even if lacking original art.

He fought to control his eyes again, to make them politely meet the girl's instead of embracing her figure as if she was only another possession, like the paintings, to be admired.

"Master Franklin will join you directly," said Lucinda smiling at Skyler. "He asks if you'll have some refreshment?" She indicated a sideboard with several crystal decanters. "May I make you a julep, suh?"

Skyler was still very thirsty, though juleps were nasty things to his taste. Lucky had managed to guzzle four beers while he'd only gotten a swallow of one, and now his throat was drier than ever. "Um," he said, still holding his hat like a beggar boy. "Would a beer be possible...?" He caught himself before adding, "Miss." *What the devil was wrong with him?* Then he heard his voice again, speaking without his permission. "It's Skyler... please."

Were the girl's eyes amused, he wondered? Or, was that a sparkle of interest?

"Certainly, Skyler. I'll be right back."

"Um?" he asked as she turned to leave. "'Scuse my ig... I mean,

25

pardon me... but are you related to Lucky?"

Again the girl's eyes may have been amused. "We're fraternal twins."

"Oh," said Skyler, abusing his hat. "I... just wondered."

"I'm sure you noticed the family resemblance, though Lucky is quite a bit larger these days."

"Um... oh, yes. Indeed he is."

"You're an ass!" muttered Skyler again, after Lucinda left the room. "You're worse than an ass! You're an... I don't know what!" He saw his reflection in a large oval mirror and actually searched his back for an arrow! "ASS!" he muttered.

Chapter Five

There was another rumble of thunder, still far away though closer now, and the glass decanters rattled their stoppers in sympathetic vibration. The room was rapidly darkening as clouds massed over the house. Skyler parted the window drapes, which, unlike those in his home, didn't spill onto the floor in decadently useless "wastes." He was scanning the gray southern sky when there was another lightning flash and he saw a gleaming reflection; something on a wall behind him mirrored in the window like a Magic Lantern picture. He turned around as the light died away to see a softly shining sword.

It was a real sword, he saw, not merely a cutlass or cavalry saber but a long, heavy sword like a knight would have borne. He'd seen many pictures of ancient swords but never one in real life, and crossed the room to admire it. It hovered above him from pegs on the wall, its brown leather scabbard armored with brass also on display below. Skyler had read quite a bit about swords, and as a child had wanted one, and saw that, although it was finely crafted, was meant for battle, not for court. A "working knight's" blade, he decided. And, though it appeared well cared-for, highly polished and lightly oiled, there were notches along its four-foot length as if it had served its purpose in life.

Again there was a lightning flash, and the sword leapt into silver brilliance. He wouldn't have taken the liberty of actually taking it down, but reached up a finger to touch it.

Then he heard slow heavy footsteps, and turned to see what might have been the fattest man on the planet.

27

In a white linen suit and with snowy white hair, Seth Franklin made Skyler think of a ship under full and majestic sail. In contrast to a spotless shirt, the man's face and hands were deeply tanned... dramatically darker than Skyler's skin after spending a year in the city.

Conscious of his common clothes and his hat with its crude decorations, Skyler hastened to meet the huge man. Shaking his hand was a little awkward because of his incredible size. The man's brown eyes studied Skyler with interest from what seemed the top of a snow-covered mountain.

"I'm honored, Master Knight," said Franklin, in a booming voice well matched to his girth. "And I've heard of your travels. A year in 'Orleans has agreed with you."

Skyler felt rather proud to be chubby in the presence of someone so large. "There was surely no shortage of good things to eat, and I believe I devoured my share, sir."

"Good food is one of life's purest pleasures and one that man has not yet perverted, though doubtless he will in time. ...You are interested in swords, Master Knight?"

"Very much, sir," said Skyler.

Franklin forged ponderously to the wall. "I'm afraid this weapon is rather plain. Not made for impressing ladies at court."

"I had divined that, sir," said Skyler, trailing along beside the great man like a dinghy beside a ship of the line. "But I'd venture to say it has slain a few dragons."

Franklin gave him an interested look. "Perhaps, metaphorically speaking, sir. But indeed it has done that for which it was made. ...Would you care to hold it?"

"Very much, sir."

Franklin took down the silver blade, and Skyler grasped its leather-wound hilt, surprised by the weapon's considerable weight. He'd intended to pose as he'd done as a child with his wooden sword made by Jupiter, but found he needed both hands.

Franklin chuckled. "It does require a bit of an 'arm,' though mostly diligent practice to wield. These were called, commonly, 'bastard swords,' though more politely 'hand-and-a-halfs,' being smaller than two-handed blades but larger than those intended for one. They were often given to men of your age, who did use both hands."

"I see," said Skyler, getting a better balance and grip. "Was this in your family, sir?"

"A distant ancestor of mine once bore it on a quest."

"What was he questing for, sir?"

Franklin smiled. "The usual things a knight searches for... honor, truth, perhaps to right wrongs." Then his face seemed to darken a bit with the dimming light in the room. "Human beings have made much 'progress' in finding new ways to slay one-another. With a gun, one needs only a fairly good eye and a finger to pull a trigger. And one may kill from a distance without ever having to face his foe."

"That's true," said Skyler. "And perhaps sad."

"But much more efficient."

Skyler relinquished the sword, and Franklin placed it back on the wall. Then Skyler stated his reason for coming and Franklin thundered a laugh.

"Lucky's a little rascal all right! I really don't know why I keep him. I swear he eats his own weight every day. He's slower than molasses in winter, and as useful as a three-legged mule."

Skyler felt embarrassed as Lucinda returned with two mugs on a tray... Lucky was her brother, and family did mean something to slaves, even if many masters denied it. "Well..." he said. "He seems like a very intelligent boy." He glanced at the girl as she offered the tray. Did her eyes seem amused again?

Lucinda asked, "Will there be anything else, Master Franklin?"

"I expect we'll be wanting more beer in a bit. And Master Knight will be staying the night so please prepare a room."

"Very good, sir," said Lucinda.

"Oh," said Skyler. "Pardon me, sir, but I got... I must be getting home." Thunder rumbled again as he spoke, and lightning reflected off the sword.

"I will not hear of it, sir," said Franklin. He moved to the window and drew back the drapes. "It will be raining like Noah's flood before you could reach the main road."

Skyler could hear the wind rising, bending the stalks of cane in the fields and whipping tree branches to and fro with their ragged streamers of flailing moss. The slaves had all disappeared and were probably snug in their cabins. "But, my parents will be worried, sir."

"My stable boy can take them a message." Franklin turned to Lucinda. "Please tell little Danny to saddle a horse."

Skyler wouldn't have called Danny "little" -- or Lucky a "little" rascal -- but supposed that was relative to Frankin's majestic size.

The sky had darkened to gunmetal gray, and raindrops exploded against the glass with a crackling sound like pistol shots. There was another lightning flash, followed by a roar of thunder that rattled the row of decanters again.

"I'll go tell Danny, sir," said Skyler, setting down his beer untasted. "No need for Lu... your girl to get wet."

"This way, Master Knight," said Lucinda, leading Skyler into the hall.

"Um, my name is..."

Lucinda laughed. "I couldn't call you Skyler in front of my master, could I?"

"Of course," agreed Skyler as they crossed a shadowy dining room and entered the kitchen in back of the house. A gust of wet wind blew back Skyler's hair as Lucinda opened an outside door. It was already raining buckets and barrels, big fat drops that flattened the lawn and splattered the bricks of the whistling walk that led to the little cook house. Steam was swirling up from the ground, though the air was still heavy and hot.

"There's the stable," said Lucinda, pointing toward some tossing trees. "But you'll be soaked to the skin!"

"It's only water," said Skyler in a tone he hoped sounded gallant. He clamped on his hat and ran for the stable across the rain-flattened grass where puddles were deeply forming. This was the first time in nearly a year he'd actually tried to run, and he found his body bobbing about like jelly being shaken. A button popped loose on his trousers, and he had to hold them up with a hand. Still, it felt good to be out in the rain, somehow wild and savagely free with the wind whipping him and tousling his hair. A razor of lighting slashed the sky, and thunder crashed like a cannon blast. In seconds he was thoroughly soaked. He stumbled, panting, into the stable, where rain rattled loud on the cedar shake roof. There were good smells of horses and hay, and Jupiter had the buggy inside. Their own nervous horse was safe in a stall, and Jupiter was soothing her. The stable boy had lighted a lantern, and was comfortably sprawled on a pile of straw with another big chunk of cornbread and honey.

Skyler stripped off his sodden shirt. "Juppy, we'll be stayin' the night. I'm sure they'll make you comfortable." He glanced at the empty buggy. "What happened to Lucky?"

"We unload him back at the Quarters," said Jupiter.

Skyler turned to the stable boy. "Sorry, Danny, but you have to ride out to my place an' tell my folks I'm stayin' here."

"Y'all 'spect they feed me?" asked Danny, and got to his feet, almost losing his trousers; the only thing retaining them -- as also applied to Lucky -- was all his pendulous frontal fat, rather like a belly bib.

"'Course they will," said Skyler. "We treat... servants right."

Lightning flashed again, glaring bright through cracks in the walls, and Jupiter calmed the skittish horse as thunder shook the building. Wind rattled the shakes overhead and rain pounded resoundingly as Danny saddled a big plow horse who didn't seem disturbed by the storm. The beast, Skyler noted, was also fat -- the fattest horse he'd ever seen -- and the saddle's cinch could hardly be buckled beneath its tremendous barrel of belly. Danny's own belly hung down so far he couldn't raise a leg high enough to get a foot in the stirrup. Skyler tried to boost him up, but couldn't lift Danny's wobbly weight, or even get a grip on the boy.

"*Déjà vu!*" he panted.

Danny giggled, more or less in Skyler's arms but spilling over everywhere. "Y'all mean tryin' to lift my brother?"

"Oh," said Skyler. "I might have known he was your brother." Finally he dropped to his hands and knees so Danny could stand on his back -- which felt about ready to break -- and pull himself into the saddle. Even then it took lots of struggle to get the fat boy aboard the fat horse.

"Y'all *sure* they feed me?" Danny panted, at last astride the massive steed.

"You tell 'em I said to give you a feast." Skyler adjusted the stirrups to fit Danny's chubby bare feet, then went to his bag in the back of the buggy and pulled out an oilskin cloak. "Wrap this around you, Danny. An' here's a dollar for your trouble."

Danny clamped his cap on tight. "Ain't no trouble as long as they feed me."

"Y'all be careful now." Skyler opened one of the doors and held on as the wind tried to slam it. The hissing rain pelted his chest and face as the hugely fat horse waddled out in the storm and splashed away through puddles. Skyler remained in the doorway, letting the wind and rain lash his body, which felt rather good after all the day's heat.

"I's sorry about your home-comin', Sky," Jupiter said, coming over. "You was right about me fallin' asleep. If I hadn't, then none of this would have happened."

Skyler thought of Lucinda, then slowly said, "I'm rather glad it happened."

Chapter Six

"What do you think of slavery, sir?"

Skyler was thinking about Lucinda -- she'd been haunting his mind all evening like a very agreeable spirit -- and it took him a moment to realize what Franklin had actually asked. His slowness wasn't surprising; he'd never been so stuffed in his life! He was sprawled in a comfortable armchair, his carpet-slippered feet on a hassock, one hand holding a snifter of brandy, a fine fat cigar in the other, while Franklin filled a gigantic chair that must have been specially made. An Argand lamp glowed on a table, providing a soft golden light, while the wind howled outside like a prowling beast and raindrops rattled the windows.

But, in here it was warm and dry, and the conversation agreeably pleasant... or had been up to this moment. Skyler glanced at an Ormolu clock above a huge fireplace. It was almost 10:30. He hoped "little" Danny had reached his house and was also warm, dry and well-fed.

Supper had been a gourmet's delight. Franklin lived alone at Content – except for his slaves, of course -- his wife had passed-on a few years ago, and his son was a lawyer in New Orleans. The table had only been set for two, but there had been enough food for ten, and the courses seemed endless in number. Skyler couldn't remember them all, only that each had been meteoric. There had been ham with a sweet honey glaze, along with fried chicken deliciously spiced. Also juicy slabs of beef, mashed potatoes and rich brown gravy, corn-on-the-cob slathered with butter, greens and tasty vegetables. He couldn't have refused anything; that would have been impolite. Besides, it was next to impossible with Lucinda seemingly always beside him refilling his beer mug and piling his plates.

He'd caught a glimpse of Lucky through the kitchen doorway; the boy had been all shiny and wet from frequent trips to the cook-house to fetch more fabulous food. He was also eating constantly, which also wasn't surprising.

Dessert had been slices of pecan pie smothered with sweet whipped cream, and Skyler could barely get out of his chair when Franklin suggested cigars and brandy.

Lucky had then appeared, dripping rainwater over the floor, and accompanied Skyler and Franklin into the lamp-lit library, where Lucinda was pouring the drinks. Lucky had knelt ponderously to remove Skyler's boots for polishing: that was a normal task for a slave, but Lucky had looked amused.

Now, thoroughly stuffed and a little drunk, Skyler pondered Franklin's question. "I'm not sure what you mean, sir."

Franklin looked amused. "Perhaps, if you will consider the question, the answer may be obvious."

"...Well... One cannot say it's morally wrong, since Negroes are not human beings like us." Skyler reconsidered. "At least not *true* human beings... perhaps on a level below us, yet, of course, above the apes."

Franklin raised an eyebrow. "Is that what they're teaching in school nowadays? That certainly makes it easier to justify enslaving them. And for their owners to sleep at night. ...At least those who are 'true human beings.'"

Skyler took another sip of brandy, feeling as if he were back in school and hadn't done his homework. "Well... even if Negroes were human beings... for the sake of argument, sir... they are surely living a better life here than wild in Africa eating each other."

"Actually, sir," said Franklin. "The practice of cannibalism is rare." He gestured toward his shelves of books. "There are more cases of 'true human beings'... shipwrecked sailors and so forth... dining upon one-another than have ever been documented among the peoples of Africa. The practice, sir... and still rare... is more common in the Dutch East Indies."

"...Oh," said Skyler. "What about head-hunters, sir?"

"They do not eat their victims. The heads are merely trophies of war, as a few of our Indian tribes take scalps. ...As did some European invaders... who still take scalps in our south-western regions."

"...Oh," said Skyler again, feeling uneasily out of his depth and wishing Franklin would change the subject. "But we need slaves," he finally said. "How else could we get things done in our country? We have crops to grow and railroads to build, and of course we must progress."

Franklin took a sip from his glass and flicked cigar ashes into a tray. "I beg to differ, Master Knight, on the point of needing slaves. If I may say, and with all due respect, I have studied the matter while you, sir, have not. And, setting aside the moral question, slavery simply *does not work*... as all great civilizations have found."

Skyler felt stunned for a moment, then said, "I feel I must disagree, sir."

Franklin smiled. "Of course you feel you must, because that is what you've been taught."

"But, consider, sir," said Skyler, and paused to wave his cigar around. "We are sitting here in a very fine house after enjoying a wonderful supper, and slavery made it possible."

Franklin shrugged. "At its very best, sir... if one may say there is a 'best'... it only works for a very short time in terms of Historical reckoning. Often just in the first generations when slaves still hope for a chance to escape and return to lands and lives they remember. Then it is in their own best interests to serve their temporary masters as if they were merely imprisoned, staying alive and remaining strong while nurturing hope of regaining freedom. But, when children are born into slavery and have no culture except that of slaves, the system begins to break down, though it may take several generations before it completely collapses."

Skyler, uncomfortable now and confused, fortified himself with more brandy. "With all respect, sir, I certainly see no evidence of our system breaking down."

Franklin looked amused again, reminding Skyler of Lucky somehow. "Perhaps you have not yet learned what to see. Or perhaps what to look for. But I assure you, sir, that our system is on the verge of collapse. One may debate in decades how long it may still survive, but any system dependent on slaves is *always* doomed to fall; and all *truly* great societies eventually learn this lesson. And those that do not invariably fall, as History has repeatedly shown."

Franklin sipped from his glass again. "Once more, disregard the moral issue and consider only the practical: having captive and unwilling workers forced to labor without any hope of betterment or personal gain, goes entirely against human nature. The work is usually not done well, and never efficiently. *All* human beings... I will not discuss the 'animal question' because frankly, sir, and with all due respect, I believe it to be beneath contempt... share the same basic needs and desires. These are food, shelter, a family life, and... absurd as it may seem to those with an inhuman grasp of humanity... a certain degree of happiness and a sense, at least, of free will and choice. Granted, that choice may only be to either work or starve, but even that is a choice. From a purely Capitalistic view, it makes far more economic sense to pay a man in exchange for his labor and then have done with him. ...To let *him* worry about where he will sleep and how he will feed his wife and children, than to have to provide him with food, shelter, and some degree of physical care to assure his continued but unwilling labor."

Franklin puffed more smoke. "And *far* better, sir, to treat that man with dignity as a fellow human being. A man who is grateful for his job and well-rewarded for doing it... a man who may even like what he does... will always do it well. More so, he will find better ways to do it, which benefits his employer." Franklin crushed out his cigar. "Slavery, sir, is not only wrong, and a damnable shame to any nation, but it simply does not work... as the South may hopefully realize before it is too late."

Skyler felt he should be arguing. His eye caught the gleam of the sword on the wall, reminding him of ancient things. "What about the Egyptians, sir? They had generations of slaves to build pyramids and their many great works."

"Their system evolved," said Franklin. "Their slaves were offered incentives to work... to do their jobs efficiently... and could often buy their freedom. Or freedom, at least, for their children. Rome evolved a similar system. And surely you must have noticed that we are evolving such a system when you were down in New Orleans? But such evolution indicates that a system of slavery is breaking down... or at least the masters are realizing that it cannot be much longer sustained. This may mean the society is becoming more enlightened. Or... and as I fear in ours... it indicates decadence. And decadent cultures do not survive."

Skyler felt his cheeks growing warm: he'd heard such theories in New Orleans -- at least in Bohemian coffee-houses -- and his father had warned against listening to them. Again he waved his cigar around but kept his tone gentlemanly, mostly in fear his voice would break into the squeak of a querulous child. "With all respect, sir, it seems to be working here at Content. You are obviously prospering, and I only assume you do not prosper more simply because you *are* content."

He wasn't sure that had come out right, but added: "And, may I say, sir, that never in my entire life have I seen such contented slaves."

He might have left it at that, but the brandy had made him bold. "Although I must add they seem a bit casual in doing their work, and there are some... my father, perhaps... who might say that your younger slaves are not over-cautious in speaking their minds. ...Still, it seems obvious, sir, that whatever system you have evolved is certainly working, and working well."

Feeling as if he had scored a point, Skyler raised his glass. "And I would be very grateful, sir, if you would explain that system to me."

Franklin studied Skyler, his smile like Lucky's again. "Perhaps we will discuss my system... as the Buddhists say, when the pupil is ready."

Chapter Seven

Franklin gazed at the sword on the wall, a handsome thing despite its scars. "Life, Master Knight, is the greatest quest a human being will undertake, though it's really a series of smaller quests which may lead us to truth... *if* truth is truly what we seek and we are brave enough to face it." He glanced at the clock. "I've enjoyed our conversation tonight, but it's getting late, don't you agree?"

"Certainly, sir." Skyler snubbed out his cigar. Then he looked up as Lucinda came in with a candlestick. He hoped she hadn't been listening -- slaves often did -- though the sounds of the storm might have muffled his justifications for slavery. Her smile appeared as bright as ever, her ebony eyes meeting his for a moment. Nevertheless, he regretted saying that Negroes weren't true human beings. He'd questioned that concept himself this year; but Franklin had been right to say that believing it probably let him sleep better.

"May I show you to your room, Master Knight?"

Skyler struggled to get to his feet against the bulk of his overstuffed belly and followed Lucinda into the hall after bidding goodnight to Franklin. He searched for something to say as they climbed a staircase to the second floor. "Um... that was a very fine supper, Lucinda."

For a moment the girl looked amused; another "Lucky expression." But, after all, they were twins. "I'll tell mother you approved."

The hall was brightly lit for an instant as lighting flashed outside a window and thunder boomed again. Lucinda led Skyler into a room and lighted a lamp with her candle. The room was large, and the lamp's soft glow left its corners in shadow. There was a gigantic four-poster bed, and a nightshirt lay on its quilted cover. Skyler's bag had been placed on a chair and his well-polished boots stood beside it... though he found himself wondering if Lucky had actually done the work.

Lucinda asked, "Will there be anything else, Skyler?"

Skyler felt stupid again, as when he'd first seen this beautiful girl. He'd heard of plantation owners who provided "companionship" for their guests, but couldn't imagine Franklin doing such a thing. Nor, he thought, would *he* have approved. "Um, no. Thank you. Good-night, Lucinda."

"Goodnight, Skyler. If you need anything, please ring." Lucinda padded into the hall and quietly closed the door.

Again there was a flash of lightning flaring through the curtains, but the thunder's crash was farther away. Rain still swept across the roof with a sizzling sound like frying eggs, but the storm was slowly passing. Skyler glanced with disgust at the nightshirt: he hated those things, like wearing a dress. He took off his clothes and sat on the bed in the state in which he'd first entered the world. He thought of Lucinda again, recalling every lush curve of her body. That awakened his own body, which, unlike his mind, was not concerned with morality.

He tossed the nightshirt onto a chair, then lay down upon the bed, sinking into feather-filled softness while the rain made shivery sounds. Suddenly, there came a laugh from somewhere in the shadows.

"Don't you know what to do with that?"

"...Lucky! How dare...!" But then Skyler found he didn't much care. After all, Lucky was only a slave.

Lucky laughed again. "One seldom accomplishes anything unless they do dare, sir." He was munching a big slice of pie, more of the pecan topped with whipped cream, and though Skyler still felt impossibly stuffed, the sight was deliciously tempting.

"Y'all want a piece?" asked Lucky. "I have a whole 'nother pie here."

"I suppose I could manage a slice," said Skyler.

Lucky got ponderously to his feet. "Suppose I could manage another myself." He waddled over and plopped on the bed, making it groan beneath his weight. His trousers were still a bit damp, and he smelled like rain with a hint of moist earth. He pulled out a jack-knife to slice the pie and gave a piece to Skyler. "Who was you thinkin' about before I interrupted you?"

"That's none of your business!" snapped Skyler. He scooted back into the pillows, and was too surprised to be annoyed when Lucky massively joined him.

Lucky smiled. "Perhaps someone you met in a house... while in New Orleans?"

"I didn't go to any houses! ... 'Least not those kinds of houses."

"Don't young noblemen have needs?"

"Don't you?" Skyler retorted.

"Why of course, sir, I'm only human."

Despite himself, Skyler smiled, and patted Lucky's ocean of belly, making it ripple in waves. "I wonder you manage."

"Where there's a will, there's always a way."

"Well, finish your pie an' get out of here."

"So you can have your way?"

"Oh, shut up."

"I thought we'd finish it together. An' have an intelligent con-versation."

Skyler patted his own belly. "I don't think I can manage more pie. I feel like you looked at the tavern today after eating all that food."

"I rubs your tummy," said Lucky. "That should help make room for more. ...Or, should I ring Lucinda to do it?"

"What?" cried Skyler, horrified, as Lucky reached for the velvet rope. Before he could think, he grabbed the huge boy. Suddenly they were wrestling like kids, Lucky trying to reach the rope while Skyler battled to hold him down. But, Lucky was four times Skyler's weight and pinned Skyler deep in the covers.

"Please!" Skyler panted, struggling but helpless beneath Lucky's mass. "Don't ring that bell!"

Lucky laughed, his nose an inch from Skyler's. "Do you implore me, sir?"

"Yes, I implore you!" Skyler gasped. "Now please get off, I can't breathe under here!"

A little while later the storm had subsided, though rain still cat-footed over the roof. The boys had finished the last of the pie, and Skyler pillowed his head on his arms. "I haven't wrestled in over a year. City boys don't know how to wrestle. Besides, it isn't gentle-manly."

Lucky laughed. "'Specially when you lose."

"You have a very weighty advantage."

"I use what I been given to do the best I can."

"So I've noticed."

Lucky produced two of Franklin's cigars and lit them from the lamp. "Buy me," he said, after blowing smoke and giving a cigar to Skyler.

"…Huh?" said Skyler, not sure he'd heard right.

"I could be your squire, Sir Knight… which would be to your advantage."

Skyler cocked his head. "How do you know about knights and squires?"

"Read about 'em, same as you."

Skyler jerked bolt upright as if he'd been struck by lightning. "You can *read?*"

"I'd think that would be obvious to one as well-read as yourself."

"…But… That's against the law!"

"Just 'cause somethin's a law don't always mean it's right… 'specially when it's made for wrong."

"Does Franklin know?"

"Franklin taught me."

"…He could be hung for that!"

"I's just black," said Lucky. "Not stupid. I have no choice of the first state of being, but many in regard to the second."

Skyler sank back on the pillow. "Change the subject. Please. …Why would you want to belong to me? You have an easy life right here. *Very* easy, from what I've seen."

"I want to see the world," said Lucky. "An' you're gonna travel.

You're gonna need a squire, Sir Knight, an' I'm just the man for the job."

Skyler cocked his head again. "What makes you think I'm going to travel?"

"'Cause knights go on quests."

Skyler remembered his childhood dreams of fighting dragons and righting wrongs. But then he sighed. "That's not very likely. I'm finished with school, and father will want me to run the plantation. ...And what if I had to put you to work? You're far too fat to do anything useful."

"Depends on what you consider useful."

"...Well... Why would Franklin want to sell you? And, at a price I could afford? ...I have some money of my own, but it's only a few hundred dollars."

Lucky laughed. "The price of a good field buck these days since you can't import us no more. But you don't seem to think I'm worth much."

Skyler smiled. "I may reconsider. But I think Franklin values you highly."

"Wonder why?" said Lucky. "I'm eatin' him out of house an' home."

"You're all doing that," said Skyler. "At least from what I've seen today. Those chubby kids just playing. An' Danny so fat he can't get on a horse."

"Come back an' talk with Franklin," said Lucky. "I think he sees some hope in you."

"What do you mean?" asked Skyler.

"Didn't he say life is a quest?"

"Were you listening?"

"I reckoned he'd say that... because he does see some hope in you."

Skyler didn't understand, but said, "Tell you the truth, I had an idea when I first came here about maybe buying your mam... mother. My father had to sell our cook, an' I guess the new one ain't very good. But of course I wouldn't ask that now."

"Why not?" asked Lucky.

"'Cause... well, it wouldn't be right."

Lucky raised an eyebrow. "You sayin' you care about our feelings?"

"...Well... maybe I do. ...At least when you deserve it."

"Buy me *and* Lucinda," said Lucky. "My sister is a real good cook, an' you wouldn't wanna bust up a set. ...An' it's right 'cause I'm askin' you to."

Chapter Eight

"**W**ell, Juppy," asked Skyler, "did you get enough to eat at Content?"

Jupiter patted his lanky middle, which looked a bit rounder this morning. "Some of the best food I's ever tasted, an' sho' nuff plenty of it, Sky."

The buggy rattled along the swamp road beneath overhanging moss-bearded trees still dripping water from last night's storm. Skyler was shirtless in his savage old hat, his boots propped on the dashboard. The air was growing hot once more, cleansed by the rain and still smelling fresh, but heavy and humid with rising steam.

Breakfast had been early, and Skyler had awakened surprised with Lucky asleep beside him when Lucinda had knocked on the door. He'd had a ridiculous thought of trying to hide the enormous boy by pulling the covers over him, but instead had only nudged him awake. Lucinda hadn't seemed surprised no matter what she might have thought... the least of which, Skyler hoped, was that Lucky merely warmed the bed, which he did very efficiently. Lucinda had brought hot water, though Skyler.didn't need to shave and probably wouldn't for several more years.

It wasn't surprising that breakfast was huge; eggs and bacon, hotcakes and sausage, slabs of buttered toast with jam, along with pitchers of foamy fresh milk. What did surprise Skyler were Franklin's clothes: the man had been dressed in plain brown trousers and a blue work shirt as big as a sail. Skyler assumed he was going out to check on his slaves; but though the sun had been up for an hour, Skyler could see them beyond the windows just beginning their work. His father would have been shocked! And the chubby children were playing again as if they had nothing useful to do. Lucinda seemed to work harder than most of the field slaves at Content -- she certainly started much earlier -- bringing in and removing plates while keeping Skyler's glass full of milk, though Lucky waddled in from the cook house, cheerfully whistling while toting more food.

"I reckon it true," said Jupiter, "what folks say about Content."

"What do folks say?" asked Skyler.

Jupiter seemed to reconsider. "Likely just foolish slave talk, Sky."

"Slave talk ain't always foolish, an' I know you don't think I am."

Jupiter looked thoughtful. "You a good young man, Sky. If they's things to be learned, you'll learn 'em, I's sure."

Skyler hadn't spoken to Franklin about Lucky's proposition last night -- best to talk with his father first before making an offer on two more slaves -- though he still didn't think he could pay the price. Franklin might have been glad to sell Lucky because he was too fat to work, but how could he manage without Lucinda, who seemed to run the house? And he wouldn't have wanted to separate twins.

The land was getting drier as the buggy drew nigh to Knight's Crossing. The road was still full of puddles -- the rather dandified buggy horse shying a bit before mincing through -- but these were fewer and farther between. The sun was becoming a demon again as it glowered down through branches and leaves, while steam ghosted up from the vine-tangled foliage.

"We could have lunch at the tavern," said Skyler. "I'll get Tom to put us a table out back."

Jupiter smiled. "I could stand to wet my whistle. Your daddy ain't as free with his beer as Massa Franklin seem to be."

"'Rewards an' special occasions,'" Skyler quoted his father, then added, "I don't want to make you uncomfortable, Juppy... an' tell me to shut up if I do... but back to learnin' what needs to be learned, y'all know somethin' about Franklin's system? Think it might work for us?"

"Don't reckon your daddy would approve."

"It surely can't be efficient," said Skyler. "Slaves havin' breakfast an hour after dawn. An' none of 'em workin' as hard as they should."

"Downright shameful, Sky."

"Don't pee on my head an' tell me it's rainin'. But, I wonder people don't talk."

Jupiter seemed to consider. "Franklin mostly keep to himself ever since his mizzus passed, an' outta sight is outta mind. But he always pay his debts on time, an' his credit be good at the bank. Content don't grow a lot for sellin', but the cane an' rice be all top-notch, an' what it do sell go out on the train to the best markets in 'Nawlins."

Skyler smiled. "Thanks for the foolish slave talk."

The buggy rattled around a bend. By the side of the road was a massive oak surrounded by tall green grass. A hugely fat horse stood in the shade taking advantage of the grass, with a very fat black boy asleep on its back.

"It's little Danny," said Skyler. "Pull up, Juppy."

The enormous horse had eaten so much its belly had broken the saddle cinch and the straps dangled down on each side. Fortunately, it just wanted to eat, or the slumbering boy would have fallen off, along with the saddle and blanket. Danny was only in trousers, and lay with his face on the horse's shoulders, his huge bottom bare to the breeze.

Jupiter set the brake as Skyler climbed down. The fat horse looked up and seemed to smile, then went on happily eating.

"Hey, Danny!" called Skyler.

"Huh?" Danny stirred, then sat up and stretched, his wobbly rolls rearranging themselves and his middle spreading around him like a blubbery torus. "...Oh. Mornin', Massa Knight."

"It's afternoon," said Skyler. "Did you get enough to eat at my place?"

"Well, yes an' no. They was surely enough, but it sure weren't the best. My sister's cookin' would put it to shame, tho' it weren't far off to begin with."

"So I've heard," said Skyler.

Danny yawned. "Stopped in town to buy me some candy with that money you give me last night. Then I had to find a black boy to help me back on my horse."

Skyler inspected the broken cinch. "You can't ride home on this, an' I don't have nothin' to fix it with."

"I can ride bareback," said Danny.

Considering the size of the horse -- its back as broad as the deck of a ship -- that seemed a likely solution. "Well," said Skyler. "You're gonna have to get down from there so we can take the saddle off. So you might as well come an' have lunch with us."

Danny smiled. "Ain't hard to reckon why Lucky likes you."

Chapter Nine

About two hours later, Skyler awoke from a full-belly doze to find the buggy nearing the gates of his father's mammoth plantation. Its name was DILIGENCE, proudly proclaimed by an iron archway cast in England a century before. The drive to the stately white Big House -- massively columned and porticoed -- was neatly graveled, freshly raked, and lined with well-trimmed shrubbery. The fields stretched away behind the house, and the Quarters were tastefully hidden by trees.

A pair of boys around Skyler's age were cutting the acre of emerald lawn with its brick-paved walks, sparkling pond, and marble fauns from Italy, all round-bellied and playing stone pipes. The boys wore shorts midway to their knees, and their midnight bodies were beautifully muscled. Skyler admired them without envy, just as he could admire the fauns: the boys had been bred for their sturdy builds, just as the fauns had been artfully carved, and all were his, or would be someday.

The boys spied the buggy and paused their work to smile and wave at Skyler. Their names were Romulus and Remus, boys he'd played with for most of his life. They had also gone swimming and fishing together, and Skyler wondered if there would be time for doing those things anymore.

A little over an hour later, Skyler was up in his room. He'd been welcomed home by his mother and father, then greeted by all the house servants. The field slaves would have the afternoon free, and a barbecue to make them grateful their future master had returned.

Skyler had been curious about what his parents' reactions might

be to all his rolly new weight, but his mother had called him cherubic, while his father had said he looked prosperous. His mother had
summoned the seamstress to measure him for new clothes, and
Skyler had finally escaped to his room, glad to be done with the fuss.
Its two large windows were open, though the drapes were drawn
against the sun. Skyler stripped out of his sweaty shirt, kicked off his
boots and yanked off his socks. His father had joked that he smelled
like a buck -- out of earshot of the servants, of course -- and soap and
water had been advised, carried in by Jupiter who offered to help
Skyler wash. Skyler had only laughed, and sent Jupiter down for a
pitcher of beer.

Skyler opened a drawer of his bureau. There were his buckskin
trousers, his favorite clothes besides his old hat. He took them out
and smiled sadly, finding them now much too small. He would visit
Jupiter's missus and pay her to make him a new pair. He found his
soft Indian boots, which still accepted his feet. He was glad he'd
outgrown his evening clothes and wouldn't have to wear them for
supper, and hoped the new cook was a little better than Jupiter had
proclaimed. He splashed some water over his chest, more to cool off
than actually wash, then began to unpack his bag.

There was a knock at the door. "Come in," called Skyler.

His father entered, tall and blond, and studied his shirtless son
for a moment. "Jupiter could give you a haircut."

"Do you disapprove of my hair?" asked Skyler. "It's always been
long an' I like it that way."

"Of course not, son." His father smiled. "But it does make you
look like a cherub, especially since you've gotten so chubby."

"One can't judge a book by its cover."

"You're no doubt a Knight beneath your 'cover,' but I was thinking of ladies your age, and of making a manly impression."

"I could beat on my chest and swing from a tree."

"A proper young lady would find that distressing."

"So I've noticed."

"Your mother is planning your homecoming party."

"I'd really rather not."

His father sighed. "I'd rather not either, but she does love her parties and we can't disappoint her." Then he smiled again. "But until I purchase a decent cook we won't be subjected to that ordeal. And I have a present for you." The man turned slightly and beckoned, and a boy peeped shyly into the room. He was dark chocolate-brown and about Skyler's age, with a newly-trimmed halo of ebony hair. He was clad in absolutely nothing, and looked and smelled carbolically clean, muscled like an anatomy model, and his teeth shone white in an uncertain smile as he gazed wide-eyed around the room. His toes, Skyler noted, were naturally spread... he'd never worn shoes in his life.

Skyler's father drew the boy in, took his shoulders and nudged him forward. "A proper gentleman of your age should have a personal servant. This is Cartwright and he's very well bred... at least physically, as you see... although he hasn't been housebroken."

"...Oh," said Skyler.

"I wanted a sturdy companion for you... you tend to be hard on fragile things, which might have included a house-bred boy. Nevertheless, I have been assured this boy is very intelligent. ...And, I certainly hope so. Frankly, I paid quite a lot for him when I should have bought a new cook."

"...Oh," said Skyler again.

His father turned the boy around, displaying a wide-shouldered, wedge-shaped back that still had a bit of a childish sway. "Not a single stripe, you see."

"...How... nice," said Skyler.

Skyler's father continued, "His master shipped him off a day early so he had to fend for himself last night, and his clothes were rather tattered. I had him bathed, of course."

"...Of course," said Skyler, recalling the handsome buck's ragged trousers at the station yesterday... for of course this was the same boy.

Cartwright had turned around again to shyly inspect his new owner.

"Well? Do you like him?" asked Skyler's father.

"...Um...Very much. ...Thank you."

"I'll let you get acquainted. Julia is working on clothes for him so yours will be a bit delayed."

Cartwright raised his amber eyes and smiled a little timidly as Skyler's father left the room. "I knowed Lucky was lucky for me!"

"...Reckon he was," said Skyler.

"...Is everthin' all right, massa?"

"...Of course," said Skyler. "Um... good to see you again, Cartwright. ...Um, please sit down. ...Would you like a glass of water?"

"No thank you, suh." Cartwright started to sit on the floor.

"No," said Skyler. "Sit on the chair. Or the bed." Feeling suddenly helpless, even trapped somehow, he went to a window and parted the drapes to look at the bright green lawn below. Peacocks strutted their rainbowy tails around the sparkling pond... one of the latest conceits. Romulus and Remus were gone, having received the afternoon free along with the other slaves. Skyler heard the pad of feet as Cartwright came up behind him.

"What wrong, suh?" asked Cartwright, reaching to touch Skyler's shoulder and apparently forgetting that to touch a white person was a whipping offense. "Don't you like me?"

Skyler turned from the window and gripped Cartwright's shoulders. "Of course I like you. ...You're just what I always wanted."

"Thank you, massa," said Cartwright.

"My name is Skyler. ...When we're alone. ...You know about stuff like that, don't you?"

"Heard tell, anyways."

"Or you can call me Sky, if you like. My friends do."

"Mean, we gonna be friends, too?"

"Well, I hope so. ...If you want to be."

"Mean, I gots a choice about that?"

"Nobody can make you be friends," said Skyler. "Even if they own you."

"You got lots of friends... Sky?"

Skyler considered that question. Jupiter was his friend. And Romulus and Remus. ...At least he'd always thought they were. He'd never *made* them be with him during what little free time they had.

Cartwright cocked his head, his bright eyes searching Skyler's. "There somethin' wrong, I can tell."

Skyler dropped his hands. "Maybe there is, but it's not you."

There was a gentle knock at the door. "Come in, Juppy," said Skyler almost gratefully.

Jupiter entered with the pitcher of beer. He'd brought two mugs, Skyler noted... all the slaves would have known of Cartwright within a few hours of his arrival. Jupiter smiled at Cartwright as he set the things on a table. "Y'all got a real good massa now, so be grateful an' please him."

"Oh, hush," said Skyler. "He don't need to hear that an' neither do I."

"Y'all wantin' anythin' else?" asked Jupiter.

Skyler turned to Cartwright. "Are you hungry? ...Don't ever be scared to say what you want."

"I could eat somethin', if that be all right. Ain't had nothin' since yesterday when you bought me that food at the tavern, suh."

"Skyler," said Skyler, glancing at Jupiter.

Jupiter smiled. "I sees what I can find."

"Um," said Skyler after Jupiter left. He'd never been good at conversation simply to make polite noise. "I presume you saw a lot of the country when you were on the train?"

"They locked me in the baggage car. Weren't no windows."

"...Oh."

Cartwright still looked uncertain, and Skyler wanted to cheer him up... though he was far from cheerful himself. He'd been planning to speak with his father about buying Lucinda and Lucky, but what was he going to do now? His father might want Lucinda to cook, but how could Skyler justify Lucky when he now had a boy of his own? Of course, none of this was Cartwright's fault.

"How 'bout a beer?" asked Skyler.

"Sho'... I means, yes, please."

Skyler poured the two mugs full and handed one to Cartwright. "Stop lookin' like a nervous dog about to pee on the floor. That don't please me at all."

"I can't help it, suh... Skyler. I ain't housebroke like your daddy say, an' I don't know what I's s'posed to be doin'."

"That makes two of us," said Skyler. "Sometimes I don't feel housebroke myself. But, you're supposed to be drinkin' your beer."

Cartwright obediently leaned way back and tilted the mug to his lips.

"Um," said Skyler. "You *can* take a while to enjoy it."

Cartwright smiled and wiped his mouth... he'd drained the mug in seconds. "I did enjoy it, suh... Skyler. All nice an' cool."

"Yeah, we have a deep cellar. ...Feel a little better now?"

"Yeah, Sky. ...But maybe I should have me another?"

Skyler refilled Cartwright's mug, then gulped down half of his own. Cartwright drank a little slower, but his mug was dry before Skyler's.

"I does feel better," said Cartwright.

Skyler drained his own mug, refilled it once more, then poured the last of the pitcher in Cartwright's. He watched as Cartwright guzzled it down and came up for air with a smile.

"I thinks I's gonna like it here." Cartwright burped. "'Scuse me, Sky."

"What did you do before my dad bought you?"

"Helped fix wagons an' such. Got rented out to the railroad a while."

"Oh," said Skyler, feeling a little better, too. "Guess I should start taking care of you. ...Let's see how you look in buckskin. My old trousers should fit you. ...Can you ride a horse?"

"Sho' can, Sky."

"You like to swim?"

"Sho' does, Sky. ...But, ain't you got no work for me?"

"Lots," laughed Skyler. "Startin' right now." He went to the bureau and took out the trousers. "Here's your first job, put these on. They might be a little big, but I'm sure you'll look better in 'em than me."

They were a bit big and clung very low, while almost concealing Cartwright's feet except for his widespread toes, but Skyler thought he looked very handsome. Cartwright seemed to agree, gazing at himself in the mirror.

"Ain't never had me nothin' so fine! Thank you, Sky!"

Skyler stepped back and inspected the boy. "Mother will dress you all silly, but you can wear those when you're with me. I'm getting' a new pair made."

"Then we look like twins."

Skyler laughed. "You have an imagination."

"Is that somethin' I's s'posed to have?"

"Not if you were a regular slave; it would just get you in trouble. But it's somethin' that pleases me."

"I thinks Lucky has one, too. ...But y'all didn't seem very pleased by it."

Skyler frowned a little. "I'd rather not discuss Lucky now, if you don't mind."

"Oh, no, Sky. I don't minds at all if it don't please you."

"Well, don't be scared of not pleasin' me if you got somethin' you think needs sayin'." Skyler put on his hat and hoisted his trousers. "C'mon, we'll get somethin' to eat in the kitchen an' then ride down to the river." He took his rifle from pegs on the wall -- a .50 caliber Smith -- then pulled leather pouches of caps and cartridges out of a bureau drawer. "Want to carry this, Cartwright?"

"Sho', Sky."

"Sling it over your shoulder," said Skyler. He helped Cartwright with the rifle and pouches, their leather straps across Cartwright's chest, then found his big Bowie knife in a drawer. But of course his old belt wouldn't fit.

"You might as well wear this, too," said Skyler, handing the knife and belt to Cartwright. "Otherwise you'll be goin' around with your trousers off your bottom like me."

Cartwright laughed. "Maybe we start a new style."

Chapter Ten

Jupiter was climbing the main stairs -- a majestic sweep of polished oak -- as Skyler and Cartwright descended. The old man carried a cloth-covered platter and smiled at the shirtless boys. "Found some fried chicken that's etable, tho' nowhere as good as we had at Content."

"Thanks, Juppy," said Skyler. "Help yourself, Cartwright."

The boys took three pieces each. "We're goin' down to the river," said Skyler.

"Y'all watch out for snakes," said Jupiter. "An' Jessup seen a 'gator last week, tho' they mostly don't come this far up."

The boys went out in the hot sunshine, and Skyler led the way to the stables. The sultry air seemed strangely still without the sounds of slaves at work. The blacksmith shop was deserted, a wagon wheel standing half re-spoked, the forge still smoking a little. Gone was the clang of hammers on iron, along with the clacking of clippers and shears to keep the lawns and shrubbery trimmed.

The stable boy was about eleven. He'd managed to get more than slightly drunk -- unusual at Diligence because Skyler's father was careful with beer -- and lounged half asleep in the hay bin. He scrambled quickly to his feet, though swaying a bit, when Skyler entered.

"Good to have you back, suh," he said, bowing and almost falling.

Skyler took his shoulders to steady him. "Thanks, Billy. You've grown a lot since I seen you last. This is Cartwright."

"Heard tell there was a new boy," said Billy.

Skyler smiled. "I'm sure of that."

"Pleased to meet you," said Billy, shaking Cartwright's hand. Then he turned back to Skyler. "Y'all be wantin' Judy, suh?"

Judy had been Skyler's favorite horse, but she was getting on. He looked down the long row of stalls where many fine horses waited, most with bright eyes and spirited heads, and all seeming eager to go for a ride. "That's all right, thank you, Billy. You're supposed to be havin' a free afternoon. Tell Jupiter I said to give you some more beer."

"Thank you, suh!" The boy trotted off, weaving a bit.

"Ain't rode more than middlin' much," said Cartwright, finishing his last piece of chicken and tossing the bone out the door. "My ol' massa was careful 'bout that since we had us a couple runaways."

"Were they caught?" asked Skyler.

"Yeah."

Skyler almost said he was sorry – they'd surely been savagely whipped and branded -- but showing sympathy wouldn't be proper. He started along the line of stalls, where large dark eyes regarded him, but ignored the row of riding horses and continued past the carriage beasts. There were larger stalls down at the end where the work and wagon horses were kept. Skyler stopped at a gigantic horse who was even huger than Danny's fat mount, except its mass was composed of muscle. Its hooves looked as big as barrel-heads, its back as broad as a railroad car, while the tips of its ears brushed the stable's rafters. Like most of his kind, he was gentle... maybe resigned to a life of toil. His shiny brown eyes looked curious as Skyler pulled the wooden pin and opened the gate to his stall.

Cartwright drew back in awe. "I never seen a horse so big!"

"He's a Clydesdale," said Skyler. "My father had him shipped from Scotland to pull our new mechanical reaper. That machine does the work of twenty slaves. ...Mind your feet," he added, as the mammoth horse ambled out of the stall. "If he steps on yours he'll mash 'em flat. ...Find a bridle. A big one. Over there in the tack room. We'll have to ride him bareback 'cause there ain't no saddles made his size."

"How we gonna get up there?" asked Cartwright, returning with the bridle and gazing at the enormous beast. "That be like tryin' to climb on the moon!"

"We'll stand on that rail. C'mon."

The horse looked over a shoulder when the boys were finally astride his back. He seemed more surprised than anything else -- no one had ever ridden him -- though he probably didn't notice the weight. He clopped calmly out in the sunlight after Skyler nudged him with his heels, and the boys had to duck to clear the doorway.

"I don't think we'll go for a gallop," said Skyler as the huge horse placidly ambled along, seeming to shake the earth with each step.

"I'd sooner not," said Cartwright. "It a long ways to the ground!" His arms were tight around Skyler's waist, hands clasped beneath Skyler's belly, though after a while he relaxed a little.

They passed near the edge of the Quarters. The ancient cabins were built of logs, most a hundred years old, and looked like tumble-down hovels compared to the Quarters at Franklin's plantation. The barbecue was in progress, and the scent of pork roasting made Skyler's mouth water. A cart held two wooden kegs, and beer was sparingly being dispensed by one of the trusted house boys, who was looking more than a bit supercilious among the common slaves.

Skyler studied his property: none were unhealthily skinny, and a few of the youngest kids were chubby, not having been put to work as yet; but compared to the slaves he'd seen at Content he wouldn't have called them overly fed. The men and boys were mostly muscle, but they had been bought or bred for strength. Remus and Romulus waved at Skyler, as did most of the others, properly grateful -- at least outwardly -- for this free afternoon. But, he noticed one sulky face with eyes that met his with sullen defiance... a brawny boy of maybe sixteen. Skyler committed that face to mind as the horse ambled on beneath trees toward the river.

A few minutes later they arrived at an oxbow lagoon cut off from the river at this time of year. The water looked cool and inviting shaded by oak and cypress trees. A few naked slave boys were swimming, laughing and splashing, enjoying themselves. They stopped their play when the huge horse appeared, but then saw Skyler and ran to meet him, greeting him with smiles and grins, then gathered around to inspect Cartwright. All seemed impressed that he carried the rifle along with Skyler's knife.

"Is the food ready, suh?" asked the oldest boy.

"Smells just about," replied Skyler. "Y'all better run before it's gone."

The kids dashed back up the path as Skyler slid to the ground. He landed rather awkwardly, still not used to all his new weight, while Cartwright grounded as light as a cat. Skyler tied the reins to a tree and left the horse in a shady spot, then slipped off his trousers and pulled off his hat, hanging them on a bush.

Cartwright smiled. "Never seen a white boy naked. ...I means a young mas..."

Skyler laughed. "We're alone."

Skyler and Cartwright swam for a while, then Skyler gave Cartwright a shooting lesson, showing him how to load the big rifle with cartridge and percussion cap. Cartwright's aim was remarkably sharp, and Skyler patted his shoulder after he'd clipped a twig from a tree. "You'll be as good as me in a week. An' that ain't too bad, if I say so myself."

Cartwright lowered the smoking gun. "Y'all the best massa I ever had."

"Thanks, but you hardly know me. ...You've had more than one other master?"

"I was sold a couple times. First when I was a baby. Don't remember my mammy at all."

"Oh," said Skyler, feeling sad, though that wasn't proper.

Cartwright cocked his head and listened. "There somebody else goin' swimmin' somewheres?"

Skyler pointed. "Yonder's a creek beyond the trees with another swimmin' hole. But it's only for girls an' you'll get your butt whipped with a willow switch if you're ever caught spyin' on 'em. It's one of our rules at Diligence to keep control of breedin'." Skyler laughed. "Jupiter switched my behind a few times when he caught me peepin' there. ...'Course, I was a lot younger then."

Cartwright's mouth dropped open. "He did?"

"And it hurt."

"But, can't you breed anytime you want?"

"You mean 'improvin' the stock?'"

"My last massa done that."

"Well, we don't at Diligence. But, ain't no harm in lookin'. ...C'mon. Just leave the rifle here."

"But, what about the rule, Sky?"

Skyler laughed. "Now I'm old enough to call it inspecting my property. ...C'mon, this way. An' be quiet. Pretend you're an African boy in the jungle. I used to pretend that a lot when I wasn't playin' at bein' a knight."

"Playin' at night?" asked Cartwright.

"I'll explain another time. C'mon."

Both still naked, Skyler led Cartwright along a faint path – naturally there *was* a path, used by both sexes to peep at each other -- that snaked through the vine-tangled trees. The sounds of girlish laughter and splashing grew more distinct as the boys crept along, careful of stepping on dry leaves or twigs. At last Skyler stopped at a large oak tree and leaned against Cartwright to whisper: "You get the best vantage up there."

Skyler climbed into the tree with Cartwright close behind. Skyler crept out on a branch, and a gap in the leaves revealed a view of three ebony girls swimming in emerald water. Two were about fourteen, the third a few years younger.

Cartwright whispered, "This be worth a switchin' to see!"

"Yeah," agreed Skyler. "But don't get caught comin' here alone or then I'd have to do it. An' other slaves would be watchin' so I couldn't be very gentle."

"I understand, Sky."

Skyler pointed. "The chubby one's Julia's daughter. ...Damn, but she grew in a year!"

"I thinks she the prettiest, too," whispered Cartwright. "What's her name?"

"Angel."

"She sho' is!"

"I'll introduce you to her tonight."

"...Um... I's terrible shy around girls, Sky. Never knows what to say."

"That makes two of us," said Skyler.

"But, don't you know more words than me?"

"That's never helped when talkin' to girls, an' I never met one who knew lots of words."

"Does you know any girls? Personal like?"

"How 'personal' you talkin'?"

"More than just friendly, but not over-much."

Skyler thought of Lucinda, but it didn't seem proper to tell Cartwright that a slave girl awakened feelings in him. "There's a girl at another plantation. ...A white girl of course. Mother keeps shovin' her at me at parties, but she's more like a China doll than a person."

"What's a China doll?" asked Cartwright.

"Somethin' fragile an' easy to break. More for lookin' than touchin'."

"She pretty, Sky?"

"Her face is... if you like China dolls. Hard to tell about the rest 'cause she's always in proper clothes, of course. I saw her ankles once, gettin' out of her carriage. Reminded me of chicken feet."

"'Spect there was lots of girls in 'Nawlins?"

"...Well, no, I never," said Skyler. "If that's what you're askin'. ...How about you?"

"No I never neither. But I thinks about it a lot."

Skyler sighed. "That makes two of us." Then he smiled. "Let's take in the view an' do some thinkin'."

Chapter Eleven

T he sun was low in the western sky as Skyler and Cartwright came back down the path to the boys' swimming hole. Cartwright laughed. "This been the best day of my life!"

Skyler put on his trousers and hat, then sat on a log to pull on his boots. "'Cause of havin' no work?" He smiled. "An' bein' free to see the sights?"

Cartwright slipped into the buckskin trousers. "'Cause of belongin' to you, Sky."

"Well, it's nice to own... have you with me, Cartwright. But the day ain't over yet. I 'spect you'll like the Big House food, though I'm told it's been less than meteoric since father sold our cook."

"That fried chicken was good."

"Fried chicken is pretty hard to mess up. Jupiter taught me how to make it when he took me campin'."

"'Spect you take me campin', Sky?"

"Sure I will."

The sky was turning rose and pink, and shadows were deepening under the trees as the gigantic horse ambled home. The air was growing a little cooler, and carried the scents of roasted pork, hot buttered yams and collard greens as they neared the edge of the Quarters.

"Lord, I'm hungry!" said Cartwright. "Feel like I could eat this horse."

"You an' me both," agreed Skyler. "...Um," he added. "Supper might take some gettin' used to. I 'spect you'll have to wait on me."

"Mean till you done with your eatin'?"

"Well, that, too. But, I meant you'll have to serve me. But it's mostly standing beside my chair 'cause the house servants do all the servin'. But then you'll eat in the kitchen."

Cartwright shrugged. "Reckon that the way it be done."

"I could have supper brought up to my room so we could eat together, but this is the first night I been home so I shouldn't weasel out of it."

"I understand, Sky, it your family."

"I'll make sure you ain't standin' there hungry." Skyler laughed. "An' if you can't manage to sneak a few bites, you ain't as smart as I think you are."

"I gots to dress up like you said?"

"I'm afraid so. But I'll have Jupiter tend to that. He won't make you look like a fool."

The huge horse suddenly came to a stop as a figure lurched out from behind a tree. Skyler gripped the reins, but the horse was too big to be spooked. The shadows were rapidly darkening, and Skyler squinted his eyes, seeing the sulky-faced young buck who'd locked eyes with him in the Quarters; about sixteen and beautifully muscled in nothing but ragged trousers. He was almost too drunk to stand up. Skyler scented cheap whiskey, and saw the glint of a bottle in hand.

"You got no right!" yelled the boy, staggering closer and almost falling. The horse regarded him curiously.

"The devil you takin' about?" snapped Skyler. "Get the hell out my way an' I'll forget this nonsense."

"You ain't no better than me!" bawled the boy. "You ain't no better than any of us! You got no right to make us slaves!"

"Take the reins, Cartwright," said Skyler. "Mind the horse, though he don't seem bothered; he could step on that fool like squashin' a toad." Skyler started to slide to the ground, but Cartwright grabbed his arm.

"No, Sky! He gots a knife!"

"I see it," said Skyler, dropping to earth. He stepped to the big drunken boy, who was taller than him by a head. "Where'd you get that bottle? You know that ain't allowed."

"You got no right!" the boy yelled again, and defiantly took another drink, almost toppling backward.

"I got every right under God!" roared Skyler. He reached up and jabbed a fingertip against the boy's brawny chest. "It say in the Bible I got dominion over the beasts! An' that's what you are! Nothin' but an intelligent beast... though you sure ain't actin' intelligent now."

"Liar!' shouted the boy, though he stumbled back a step. He clutched the bottle in one hand, but the other dropped to a butcher knife, its hilt protruding from a pocket.

Skyler heard Cartwright loading the rifle, the block snapping shut on a cartridge, the clicks of the hammer thumbed to full cock... an ominous triple click sound. "No," he said without turning around. "This is a good boy, Cartwright. He's just a little drunk right now an' don't know what he's sayin'. I'm sure he'll be sorry tomorrow. ...Won't you, boy? Somebody told you those things, didn't they? Some lyin' nigger who claimed he was free an' filled your head with bad ideas. ...A nigger who's far away right now, while you're standin' here gettin' in trouble. ...Ain't that so?"

The boy said nothing, but looked confused. He stood there swaying dangerously, one hand on the hilt the knife, the other grasping the bottle.

"Talk to me," said Skyler in a gentle voice. "'' me what's troublin' you."

The boy sucked a breath. "Colored folks be free in the North. Do what they want. Live like they want. An' you can't buy an' sell us there!"

"Is that what the liar told you?" asked Skyler. "That lyin' nigger who ain't here now an' got you deep in trouble."

"Why would he lie?" the boy demanded.

"'Cause he's jealous of you."

"...Why he be jealous of me?" asked the boy, his slurred voice now sounding uncertain. "I can't leave this place! Gotta work all the time!"

"'Course you do," said Skyler. "But that's what God intended for you. It's your *purpose* in life to serve me. An' it's my purpose to take care of you."

"...But, I ain't free," said the boy.

"Freedom is just a word," said Skyler. "An', like a lot of words, it can mean a lot of things. An' some of those things ain't good."

"...What you mean?" asked the boy.

Skyler pointed toward the Quarters, the fire pit glowing cheerfully and the people gathered around it, a mouth-harp and a banjo playing.

"Look there," said Skyler, putting a hand on the boy's shoulder and turning him gently to face the scene. Skyler could have easily grabbed the knife but that seemed cowardly. "Your people don't have that up in the North. They're not *together* like that in the North. Up there you're all on your own, an' fightin' each other to stay alive. Just like here you'd work all day, but it would be in a dark factory full of great big noisy machines... machines that could tear off your arms an' legs. An' nobody would *care* if that happened! You'd never see the sun 'cause you'd be inside from dawn till dusk, an' watched like a hawk by a foreman... just like an overseer... to make sure you sweated for every penny! An' that's all you'd get for your work, a few pennies! Nobody would care if you had a bed, or a roof to sleep under at night. You'd have to manage all that by yourself. An' you'd have to buy your food. An' your clothes. It's cold up there like you just can't imagine. An' it snows in the winter. You got any conception of snow? It's cold an' wet an' freezes your bones! You'd need lots of clothes or you'd freeze to death. An' you'd have to buy wood or coal for a fire. If you got sick or hurt, you'd have to *pay* for a doctor. If you lost your job an' ran out of money, you could die of starvation... right on one of those North city streets... an' nobody would care!"

The big boy was silent, leaning on Skyler. The only sounds were his labored breaths and the distant music and laughter.

"That's how it is in the North," added Skyler. "If you don't have money you might as well die 'cause *that's* what you need you to call yourself free, even though it ain't really bein' free 'cause you'd be slavin' to earn it, workin' all day every bit as hard. than you work here for me. ...An' what about when you get old?" He patted Jimmy's strong back. "I know that's a long time away, but who would take care of you up in the North when you're too old to work anymore? When the factory owners have used up your strength and thrown you away like a worn out machine. You think they feed you when you get old an' can't make 'em money no more? You think they got a peaceful place where you can just sit in the sun like the old folk here in the Quarters? ...That sound like bein' 'free' to you?"

"...No, suh," said the boy. "...Sound like bein' a slave to money."

Skyler gripped the boy's shoulder. "That's what that nigger *didn't* tell you. An' it's just the same as lyin' when someone don't tell you all the truth."

He scanned the boy's face in the fading light. "I know you, you're Jessup's boy, Jimmy. *I* care about you, Jimmy. An' I *give* you all those things you'd have to buy in the North. An' all I ask is you stay with me an' let me keep takin' care of you, an' give me an honest day's work in return."

"I's sorry, massa!" Jimmy sobbed. He dropped his face to Skyler's shoulder, his tears running warm down Skyler's chest.

Skyler stroked the boy's back. "That's all right, Jimmy. Just give me that bottle an' knife now an' go off to bed like the good boy you are."

Jimmy reached for the knife, and Skyler saw Cartwright aim the rifle, but Jimmy offered the blade hilt-first. "Stole this from the butcher shop, suh."

Skyler took it. "Let's just say you found it somewhere. You come an' talk to me any time if you get to feelin' confused again. You say Skyler Knight told you to. An' don't you get fooled by no more lies. ...Did anybody else get fooled?"

Jimmy sniffled and wiped his face. "Was only me, suh. They had me diggin' a ditch last week, an' that lyin' nigger come out the woods 'tell me all them freedom lies."

Skyler nodded. "I s'pect he's far away by now an' tellin' those lies to somebody else to get 'em in trouble like you almost were. ...You tell anyone else about that?"

"No, suh. Just like you said, it got me confused. Weren't till I started drinkin' today it all come out like this. ...S'pose I deserves a whippin'?"

Skyler patted the big boy's head. "No, Jimmy. You just got fooled; but you won't get fooled again. Now go off to bed, I forgive you."

"Thank you, suh." Jimmy stumbled away, and Cartwright lowered the rifle. "I was scared for you, Sky!"

Skyler spit on the ground. "God-dammed Abolitionists sneakin' down here an' stirrin' up trouble! I wish they were all at the devil!" He blew out a breath and wiped sweat from his chest, then drank from the bottle and made a face. "He probably got this from some white trash... who ought to be at the devil, too! I'll shoot him on sight if I catch him! Best way to get a nigger killed is let him get hold of a knife an' a bottle!" He tossed the bottle to Cartwright, who took a drink and winced.

"Lord, that nasty!"

Skyler slipped the knife into his trousers, then sighed and adjusted his hat. "Well, that's over. An' hopefully no damage done. I'll notify the sheriff about the Abolishinist an' somebody sellin' liquor to slaves."

"I boost you back up on the horse, Sky."

"That's all right," said Skyler. "It's a fine night for a walk."

"I walks with you." Cartwright slid to earth and slung the rifle over a shoulder, then took the reins and led the horse as they walked up the path toward the Big House. For a while there were only the sounds of insects, the heavy clop of mammoth hooves, and the laughter of children in the Quarters mingled with gentle music. The boys shared the last of the bottle, both making faces each time they drank. Then Cartwright asked:

"It true what you said 'bout the North, Sky?"

"Every word, from what I know. They call it bein' industrialized."

"Guess bein' free really ain't," said Cartwright. "Only bein' a slave to money like Jimmy said." Again, although it was forbidden, Cartwright touched Skyler's shoulder. "Lucky I gots a good massa like you takin' care of me."

Skyler smiled and gripped Cartwright's hand for a moment, but then looked up at the darkening sky. "Seems like we're all slaves to somethin' in life. Or some kind of system. ...But don't ever say I said that."

"It true 'bout us bein' animals, Sky?"

Skyler sighed. "I used to think so, but I don't anymore. ...But don't you tell no one I said that, either."

Chapter Twelve

"These lamb chops seem a bit underdone," said Skyler's mother politely. She smiled across the titanic table, over an acre of snowy white cloth and past the silver candle stands, each with a dozen golden flames. "Don't you think, my dear?"

Skyler stabbed his chop with a knife. "Only on one side. On the other they would delight the devil!"

Beside him, Cartwright smothered a snicker, which seemed to be getting more difficult as he learned about meals in a master's house. He was also a liitle bit drunk, which had elevated his sense of humor and lowered his normal slave caution. He leaned on the back of Skyler's chair, his posture slack and his tummy stuck out like those of the near-naked little boys -- Tommy, eight, and Willie, nine -- who waved long-handled palm-leaf fans to provide some relief from the heat.

Jupiter had dressed Cartwright in one of Skyler's white linen shirts and a pair of Skyler's old trousers, the latter a little too large and slipping low on his hips. Jupiter had dispensed with shoes, knowing they'd only hurt Cartwright's feet. Although it was evening, the air was volcanic and made even more so by candles and lamps that flooded the huge dining room with light, and Cartwright's shirt was soaked with sweat.

As his father had said, and as Skyler was finding, Cartwright *was* very intelligent: Skyler's beer mug had been less than full when Cartwright had served him the first time, and the refills that followed grew steadily smaller, while Skyler's food was neatly arranged to hide what had gone into Cartwright's mouth between the kitchen and dining room. Skyler didn't mind, of course -- he could always have seconds, thirds or fourths -- and he minded less as the meal progressed because most of the food would have shamed a cafe in the shabbiest rural railroad station.

"Really, Skyler," his father said, though leaving his own chop unmolested. "I'm sure Betty is doing her best."

"Her best to exterminate us!" said Skyler. "This is just plain nasty!"

Cartwright seemed about to choke. His shoulders shook as he fought back a laugh, while the little fan boys were openly grinning. They wore only loincloths and turbans -- Skyler's mother was fond of Arabian themes -- and looked very cool though somewhat bored eternally waving the fans.

"Here," said Skyler, handing his mug to Cartwright. "Cleanse your palate then taste this... thing."

Skyler's father raised an eyebrow. "I don't think we need your servant's opinion."

"I'd like to have it, sir," said Skyler. He held out a pink-and-black piece of meat. "It may decide my next course of action... whether to battle or bury this repulsive object upon my plate."

"Well, suh," said Cartwright, chewing. "I does pronounce it a little nasty."

Skyler offered his mug again. "Thank you, Cartwright. Perhaps you'll want to wash away that hideously disgusting taste? I wouldn't dream of subjecting you to this foul substance allegedly mint sauce. I have tasted better things of green floating upon the surface of swamps."

"Skyler," said his father. "Perhaps you've grown accustomed to New Orleans cuisine? We are, after all, in the country."

"Actually, sir," said Skyler. "The red beans and rice are superb. The boudin sausage is excellent, and I've always liked my mashed potatoes a bit on the lumpy side. Nor do I disapprove of the gravy. The collard greens surpass themselves, and the same could be said for the corn-on-cob. But, perhaps we tax poor Betty's skills beyond her former station? I should love to sample her hog maws, and I'm sure she does wonders with chitlins."

Cartwright almost choked again, and the little boys giggled. Skyler patted Cartwright's back. "Is there something stuck in your throat, poor boy? A bit of braised hoof, or some barbecued wool? Wash it down, then fetch me another beer, please."

"Really, Skyler!" exclaimed his father as Cartwright left the dining room walking a little unsteadily. "You'll spoil that boy in a week! He's eaten and drunk as much as you, but *his* place to eat is in the kitchen *after* you have been served."

"I'm using him as my food-taster, father. Just like back in the days of yore when princes were poisoned at table. He hasn't suffered convulsions yet, which does seem to prove he's a sturdy companion."

"Perhaps we should have dessert now?" his mother suggested mildly. "Betty has made peach pie."

"Pity the peaches!" groaned Skyler.

His father pushed his chop away. A footman removed it instantly and carried it off to the kitchen.

Skyler called, "Beware it doesn't bound up and baaa! At least the half that wasn't cremated!"

"Coffee, suh?" The elderly butler tactfully asked.

"I think not, Jacob, thank you," said Skyler, as Cartwright returned with the beer. This time the mug was only half full, and Cartwright stumbled a bit.

"This was the last in the kitchen, suh." He plopped the mug in front of Skyler and grabbed the chair for support. "Y'all want me to go to the cellar?"

"Later, thank you," said Skyler, then whispered, "Pull up your trousers." He added in a normal voice, "Have you seen the pie, faithful squire?"

"I has, suh," Cartwright said solemnly. "An' I must say it look very nasty."

"Oh dear," said Skyler's mother.

"Dammit!" exploded Skyler's father, flinging down his napkin. "I won't have much more of this!"

"Beggin' your pardon, suh," said Cartwright. "But if you's speakin' about that pie, I wouldn't be havin' none of it."

Skyler gave Cartwright a poke in the side.

"Oh dear!" said Skyler's mother again. "How can I ever entertain when the food is just so..."

"Swillish?" suggested Skyler, and the little boys burst into giggles again.

"Skyler!" snapped his father, as Cartwright broke out laughing. The butler stepped quickly into the kitchen, shooing the footman ahead of him.

Skyler pinched Cartwright's arm and whispered, "Stop laughin'."

Skyler's mother went on, "I was planning your homecoming party next week."

Skyler sighed. "I'd really rather not, mother. You know I don't do well at parties, but thank you just the same."

"But, Skyler, you must!" his mother exclaimed. "How else will you meet the right people? And Daphilla is so looking forward to seeing you again."

Skyler frowned. "I'm afraid I can't say the same."

"...But she's such a nice young lady."

"Frankly, mother, she bores me to tears. And her name sounds like a disease."

"Skyler!"

Cartwright leaned close to Skyler's ear. "She the one with chicken feet?"

"Yeah," whispered Skyler.

"Skyler," said his mother. "You simply *must* have a homecoming party. It's *expected* of gentlemen your age who've gone away on travels."

"I've hardly 'traveled,' mother, as if I've been visiting castles in England or the Egyptian pyramids."

Skyler's mother paid him no mind, turning to his father instead. "Perhaps we could rent Ruthie back from the Bensons? Just for one day?"

Skyler's father looked gloomy. "I'm afraid that's impossible, dear. She was devastated at being sold, and they do have feelings you know. It would be, at least, in very poor taste... and I certainly meant no pun... to expect her to cook for us again."

Skyler's mother looked determined. "Skyler simply *must* have a party or everyone will talk."

Skyler rolled his eyes. "Then they don't have much to talk about in their dreary little lives."

"Skyler!" exclaimed his mother. "What a Bohemian thing to say!"

"Next I'll be painting pictures," said Skyler. "Or, perhaps, I shall write a poem... about a girl with fowlish feet with whom my mother insists I meet whose name sounds like a malady of bursting boils of boredom."

"*Skyler!*" cried his mother. "...And when have you seen Daph-illa's feet?"

"Once, I think, in a nightmare."

Skyler's father frowned. "Perhaps we had better change the subject." He turned to his wife. "I promise I'll make every effort to find a proper cook, dear."

Skyler said, "I'm delighted with Cartwright, sir. And I thank you with all my heart for him." He slipped his arm around Cartwright's waist, though more for support than displaying affection. "And I realize now, after seeing our table so vilely defiled, what a sacrifice you have made in giving me this wonderful boy. What is the price of a decent cook?"

"In the caliber of poor old Ruthie? Considerably more than I paid for your boy. ...But it's not so much a matter of money: it seems as if all the truly skilled cooks are down in New Orleans these days, or else aboard the riverboats." Skyler's father looked thoughtful. "Seth Franklin has an excellent cook, according to what I've heard. And his size would seem to confirm it."

Skyler took a swallow of beer. "I can attest to the skills of his cook." He wondered if this might be the time to mention Lucinda, if not Lucky, but then his mother said:

"He and his wife... bless her soul... had the grandest parties out at Content! And the food was marvelous! It was always worth that long dreary drive."

Skyler's father asked, "How is Franklin these days?"

Skyler sipped more beer. "Despite having such a small planta-tion, he seems to be doing quite well. He's devised a new system to manage his slaves. But, I don't believe it's very efficient in terms of profitable production."

Skyler's father smiled. "A year of expensive education wasn't wasted on you." He turned to his wife. "He used the words profitable and production."

"I'm sure that's very nice, dear."

Skyler went on: "Franklin and his servants seem very content with what they have... if you'll excuse a pun, sir."

"I've heard some talk," said his father. "That he's let his slaves get lazy. I saw that boy of his last night... I've never seen a child so fat! Let alone a slave! It's a wonder he's able to earn his keep!"

Skyler thought of Lucky. "Well," he said, after downing his beer. "I hope to learn about Franklin's system."

"Our own has always sufficed," said his father. "Treat your slaves well but with firm discipline." He glanced at one of the little boys. "A bit faster, Tommy, you look half asleep. ...See they're properly cared for, cull the rebellious and recalcitrant, and breed for strength and docility. We haven't had a whipping in years."

Tommy began fanning vigorously.

Cartwright reached for Skyler's mug. "Should I go to the cellar now, suh?"

"Go eat," said Skyler. "Or I should say, finish our supper."

"Yes, massa."

Skyler pinched his arm.

His father asked, "Would you like a cigar in the library, son? I'd enjoy hearing more of your thoughts on production."

Skyler glanced to the kitchen doorway, where Jupiter had appeared. The old man gave him a nod, and Skyler manufactured a yawn. "Pardon me. I didn't get much sleep last night... the storm and all. With your and mother's permission, I beg to be excused."

"Of course, son." His father glanced at Cartwright as he wavered through the kitchen doorway. "I assume you've made arrangements for him?"

"Arrangements?" said Skyler, about to get up.

"Where is he going to sleep, son? He's your responsibility now... seeing he bathes so he doesn't offend, making sure he's properly dressed... which will include shoes in the house... and training him to serve you. You'll have to look after his health... be sure he cleans his teeth and such. Keep his hair trimmed to your satisfaction. And always be sure he remembers his place. A gentleman is judged by his servant. And, often it's the servant who makes the first impression... such as Frankin's messenger. If I wasn't acquainted with the man I would have thought the worst of him for sending such an impudent boy!"

"Oh... yeah," said Skyler, thinking of Lucky again. Skyler *was* delighted with Cartwright. He wouldn't have said he would rather have Lucky -- who really was very impudent -- but of course the boys were different and each had their own qualities. "He'll sleep in my room."

"As you wish," said his father. "But not on the floor. You should have had a cot set up. And seen about his personal needs... a basin, soap, towels, a wash-cloth, a pitcher of water, a drinking glass... you surely don't want him using yours! And a separate chamber pot. All of that is your duty to him as a responsible master."

"Well," said Skyler. "He can sleep with me tonight, and I'll see to the rest tomorrow."

His father nodded. "I'd advise you to make sure he bathes again; he's been sweating like a pony all evening, no doubt unaccustomed to being indoors. Just be careful, as I've already warned, that you don't spoil your boy. There are few things more distressing to see than a servant who's over-familiar. I fear that Franklin has allowed this to happen. His stable boy... a stable boy!... was critical of his supper last night! Also of his breakfast this morning! Jacob was very upset! Had you not sent a message to treat him well I would have caned his bottom!" He glanced at the little boys, who were smiling. "You may go."

Skyler rose a bit heavily. Although the main courses had been very nasty, he'd eaten a lot of the lesser fare -- the rice and beans, potatoes and such -- and was more than comfortably full. He came around the table to kiss his mother's cheek.

"It's good to have you home, son," she said, returning the kiss. "And I'm sure you'll feel better about your party after you've gotten some rest. ...Wouldn't it be so very nice if Franklin would sell us his cook?"

Skyler's father laughed. "Fat chance of that, my dear."

Chapter Thirteen

artwright was perched on a stool in the kitchen with a plate of boudin sausage and rice, and looked up and smiled as Skyler came in. "This ain't bad, Sky. It only that fancy Big House food Betty don't know how to cook."

"I know," said Skyler. "But you can't entertain with nig... common food, an' my mother will have her parties. ...Which I wish were at the devil!"

"Can I take this shirt off now, Sky? Lord, it hot in this house!"

"Not only can you, but I insist." Skyler unbuttoned and peeled the shirt off Cartwright's glistening body, then stripped off his own to rub Cartwright down like a hard-ridden horse. "Bet you thought it was all luxury for us?"

"I learn a lot today, Sky. Y'all ain't as free as I thought you was." Cartwright thought for a moment. "Like masters be slaves to they own inventions."

"That's pretty profound... that means smart," said Skyler. "An' perceptive, too... that means you see a lot. Though the proper word is 'conventions,' meanin' ways of doin' things that most people think are proper. ...An' a few of those should be at the devil."

He poked Cartwright's stony stomach, which bulged as tight as a drum. "You keep eatin' like you did tonight, you're gonna look like me in a month."

"Well," said Cartwright, studying Skyler. "You keep goin' around out no shirt in the sun, you gonna look like *me* in a month."

Skyler laughed. "I almost did before I left. Little Miss Chicken Feet didn't approve. She's as white as a catfish belly. ...What little of her you can see, anyway."

"Is the whiter you are the better you are? Like, smarter than darker?" asked Cartwright.

"You wouldn't think so if you met her. I swear her head's so empty it echoes. Mother keeps shovin' her at me 'cause they one of the better families 'round here... 'least if you judge 'em by money. But I'll be as dark as an Indian soon an' you can tell me if I got stupid."

"Mean I can say if I think you stupid?"

"Yeah, but please don't unless I deserve it."

Skyler finished the rub-down. A minute later the back door opened and Angel shyly peeped in. She was barefoot and clad in a simple slave dress. Cartwright got to his feet in surprise, but Skyler patted his back.

"Hello, Angel," said Skyler. He held onto Cartwright, who shied back a little as Angel came in.

The girl smiled. "Evenin', Massa Knight. It good to have you home again. An' we all thank you for the free afternoon."

"Thank you, Angel. It's good to see you. This is Cartwright, my personal boy."

"Heard they was a new boy in the House." Angel came up to Cartwright, who would have shied back even more except for Skyler holding his shoulders.

"Pleased to meet you, Cartwright," said Angel.

Cartwright swallowed. "...Pleased to meet you, too, Angel."

"I can only stay a few minutes then I gotta get back to sewin'."

Skyler glanced to the doorway, where Jupiter stood outside with a lantern, and patted Cartwright again. "I'll go down to the cellar an' fetch us a pitcher of beer."

Cartwright was still on his feet when Skyler returned with a brimming pitcher. "Did you have a nice talk?" asked Skyler.

Cartwright gave Skyler a chest to chest hug, which could have been a hanging offense. "Thank you, Sky!"

"Be careful," laughed Skyler. "You'll spill our beer."

"She just as pretty in clothes!"

"I hope you didn't tell her that!"

"Ain't sure what I said, but she didn't seem to think I was stupid."

"That's a good sign," said Skyler. "Though I ain't no expert on talkin' to girls." He studied Cartwright a moment. "You two would make a real good pair. Your African features are really quite handsome. You're beautifully built an' so is Angel. I'm sure you'd have strong healthy kids."

"...Um... meanin' no offense, Sky, but couldn't I get to know her first? I means like a person instead of just breedin'.'"

Skyler laughed again. "I'm soundin' like my father! An' you're my personal boy so I'd never make that choice for you."

"That a relief to hear. ...'Course sometimes I want to breed real bad."

"That makes two of us," said Skyler.

An hour later, the boys were lying side-by-side on Skyler's huge four-post bed. The room's two windows were open and there was a breeze that cooled the leaf and earth-scented air. Muslin curtains defied insects, and fireflies danced in the darkness outside. The house was peacefully silent except for a clock somewhere in its depths faintly striking the hour of ten. The Quarters were also quiet beyond the moss-bearded trees... the slaves would have to be up before dawn.

The boys were naked and sharing more beer, drinking it straight from the pitcher. A lamp glowed on the beside table, and Skyler had been reading to Cartwright from a book about knights and chivalry.

"So, all that story be there in that book?" asked Cartwright, his arms crossed comfortably under his head upon a fluffy feather-filled pillow, his dark brown body a warm contrast to the snowy white of the sheet. "Ain't none of it in your mind, Sky?"

"That's right," said Skyler. He lay the book down and passed the near-empty pitcher to Cartwright. "'Course, some of it's in my mind 'cause I read this book a lot. An' some of it should be in your mind now so you know what knights an' squires are. That's called education. Too bad you can't read or you'd have some."

Cartwright drank and passed back the pitcher. "How come we ain't allowed to read an' get some education?"

"...Well... 'cause you'd get ideas."

"I gets 'em anyways, Sky."

Skyler paused with the pitcher to his lips. "Tell me one."

"Well... when I got rented out to the railroad I got a idea 'bout makin' the engine's headlight brighter so's the engineer could see better at night. Weren't much, just a better reflector I hammered out when I had some free time."

Skyler drank and passed the pitcher. "That was a practical idea, you can have all of those you want. I was talkin'... well, abstract ideas. ...Like, what's right or wrong. Some people call it Philosophy; real smart people who read lots of books. Like Lucky's master, Franklin. But, those ideas can be dangerous; you saw what they did to Jimmy."

"But them was bad ideas."

"But Jimmy didn't know they were bad 'cause he doesn't have education. ...See, when you have education, you know when ideas are good or bad. So if somebody tells you a bad idea you're smart enough to know it's bad an' then you don't get fooled."

"But, if Jimmy had some education wouldn't he knowed them was bad ideas 'bout wantin' to be free?"

"...Let's change the subject if you don't mind."

Cartwright drank the last of the beer, set the pitcher beside the lamp and lounged back on the pillow again with his arms crossed under his head. "This truly been the best day of my life! Thank you, Sky."

"Well, you're a real good boy," said Skyler. "An' I'm lucky I got you." He was about to pat Cartwright's head, but that didn't seem like enough, so he lay a hand on Cartwright's chest. "You been thinkin' of Angel?"

Cartwright smiled. "She be in my mind, for a fact, 'long with them knights you read me about, but in a different way. Is she in your mind, too?"

Skyler thought of Lucinda, but said, "Not in the way she might be in yours. After all, she's a slave."

"Guess you don't find her pretty 'cause of her color an' African features."

"'Course I find her pretty," said Skyler, also lounging back and crossing his arms under his head. "A sunny day can be pretty, with the water sparkling in the bayou an' everything green an' the sky blue above. But so can a night with the moon all silver an' stars like diamonds across black velvet."

"Ain't that a Bohemian thing to say?"

Skyler cocked his head. "How you know what's Bohemian?"

"'Cause of what you said at the supper table 'bout paintin' pictures an' writin' poems."

"You know what a poem is?"

"A song out no music." Cartwright considered. "Bohemian sound like seein' the pretty in things most people don't think are pretty. ...Or maybe never thought was pretty till somebody painted a picture or wrote a poem about 'em."

"That's pretty profound," said Skyler. "An' you're right; some people never look for pretty, an' some been taught some things ain't pretty even though they are."

"Kinda like bein' a slave to conventions." Cartwright smiled. "Who be in your mind when... well, you know?" He made a hand gesture over his shaft, which, like Skyler's was lazily lolling. "Sho'ly not little Miss Chicken Feet."

Skyler laughed. "Surely not! I'm supposed to think she's pretty 'cause that's a convention, too, but I don't see no pretty in her."

"'Cause you got education?"

"...Well... yeah. But that's not the kind of education that comes from readin' books. ...Guess you could call it life education; knowin' if somethin' is pretty or not based on what you've seen in life."

"An' what bad or good?"

"Yeah."

"Don't I got that kind of education?"

"'Course you do," said Skyler. Then he thought for a moment: there had been lots of girls in his mind -- though most had been imaginary -- and sometimes he didn't need them to do what had to be done. But all he could picture now was Lucinda, though it seemed disrespectful to think about her in that kind of context. He forced a shrug. "Lots of times I just do, I don't think. Don't you?"

"Sho', Sky, lots of times."

"Um, you feel like doin' it now?"

Cartwright smiled. "Be nice havin' nothin' to do but that, an' lots of time for doin' it."

"...Oh yeah," said Skyler. "I guess you never had much free time."

"Yeah, or else I was just too tired."

"I know seven different ways."

"You does?" said Cartwright. "I only knows two."

"I had lots of free time to learn 'em."

"'Spect you got time to teach me a few?"

"Bet you don't know this one," said Skyler.

Chapter Fourteen

A faraway clock in one of the parlors -- Skyler had forgotten which one -- slowly began chiming twelve. The boys lay side-by-side again in the glow of the lamp turned low, their heads once more pillowed on arms, their bodies glistening with sweat. Cartwright sighed. "Never had time to do more than two."

"Which one did you like the best?" asked Skyler.

"The last one was pretty good."

Skyler laughed. "That was your idea, an' I agree."

Cartwright yawned. "Ain't stayed up this late since I worked on the railroad."

"What did you do?" asked Skyler.

"They had me layin' track at first, but then they put me to polishin' bugs off the engines' headlights at night when they come in to a station."

"That sounds fairly easy."

"Well, they was other stuff, too; them passenger cars got big chamber pots."

"...Oh," said Skyler, then also yawned. "I left word not to call me till ten in the mornin'."

Cartwright smiled. "I does like belongin' to you, Sky."

"Don't get spoiled. I'm usually an early riser."

"I has been, too."

Skyler sighed. "An' I'll probably have to start gettin' up early to ride out an' check on the slaves. No doubt father will want me to."

"Ain't that what overseerers for?"

"*Quis custodiet ipsos custodes*," said Skyler. "That's Latin. Means,

82

'who will guard the guardians,' or 'who will watch the watchers.' There's a lot of work in bein' a master... though I'm sure it don't look that way to slaves."

He thought for a moment, then added, "My family wasn't wealthy when we first came here, an' we didn't get where are today without a lot of hard work. That's why this place is called Diligence, which means hard work an' watchfulness. It's natural for slaves to get lazy if they're not watched all the time. An' the watchers get lazy if they're not watched. ...Of course that applies to anyone who has to work for somebody else."

"Don't seem like Lucky gets watched a lot."

"No it don't," said Skyler. "An' that perplexes me a bit... that means it makes me curious in a troubled kind of way."

Cartwright cocked his head. "It troubles you 'cause a black boy is lazy, even if he ain't yours?"

"It sets a bad example for other people's slaves. ...Like when you met Lucky yesterday at the railroad station; didn't you wonder how a slave boy could have gotten so fat?"

"It did rouse my curious some," said Cartwright. "Tho' I wouldn't say it got me perplexed. But we wasn't talkin' long. He was there when they put me off the train, sendin' a telegram for his massa."

"How did he get to town?" asked Skyler. "He's far too fat to have walked from Content... though I've noticed he gets around quite well when it's in his own interest to do so."

"Come in on a wagon-load of rice. 'Spect he was gonna ride it home after the rice unloaded."

"Which of course he wouldn't be helpin' with."

"Said his massa give him a day..."

Skyler laughed. "An' a nickel to buy some candy. ...I'll give you the same anytime you want."

"I like bein' with you, Sky."

"If you ever want to be alone or have a free day for yourself, don't be scared to tell me."

"Don't know what I do with a whole day all alone by myself."

"Well, you could eat an' sleep, an' do a lot of what we just done. Or you could read a book... oh, sorry."

Cartwright laughed. "Guess I could think one up."

Skyler frowned a little. "But what perplexes me more is how Franklin apparently makes a profit when none of his slaves seem to work very hard. 'Least from what I seen out there. ...An' Lucky ain't the only fat one, you should see his 'little' brother!"

He told of his visit with Franklin, then added that Lucky had asked to be bought, along with his sister Lucinda. "Which *really* perplexes me," he finished.

"Guess I messed it up for you, Sky. Now you can't buy him 'cause you got me."

"You didn't mess up nothin'," said Skyler. "An' don't you ever go thinkin' that. ...Besides, why would I want him? What purpose could he serve? ...An' he'd give you bad ideas."

"Maybe you could educate me so's I knows bad ideas when I hear 'em?"

"I have to educate you a little 'cause of you bein' my personal boy. ...An' I want to 'cause I like you. ...But, I don't know what I'd do with Lucky... assuming I could afford him. At best he'd be like a pet; something without any purpose in life."

"Does everthin' gots to have a purpose? Can't some things just... well, just be? Like paintin's an' poems. An' sun on the water an' stars in the sky?"

"Well, yeah," said Skyler. "Those kinds of things... they make life better. Some people say they uplift the soul an' make human beings more human." Then he laughed. "But would you call Lucky one of those things?"

Cartwright smiled. "He might just be a nice thing to have for all them reasons you just said. An' even a pet gots a purpose in life if he make his master happy."

Skyler was quiet a moment or two, listening to the gentle night sounds, then he began to talk of Lucinda. He spoke of her cooking at first, but slowly came round to describing her... her cute dimpled smile, her lush full figure, her satiny skin, and the look in her eyes when she spoke to him.

"She sound real nice," said Cartwright. "Like pretty poems an' pictures."

"She is," said Skyler. "But, maybe I shouldn't have told you all that."

"I can keep a secret, Sky."

"Yeah, I know you can."

Cartwright added, "An' she can cook, so she gots a purpose. ...If everthing gots to have one."

"I didn't say everything," said Skyler.

"You wouldn't wanna bust up twins, so that be a purpose for buyin' 'em both." Cartwright smiled again. "An' I thinks you like Lucky, too... maybe like likin' a picture."

"Strange as it seems, I do rather like him. But pictures don't eat or have to be clothed, an' Lucky requires a lot of both. He'd have to be dressed for the house, an' to travel with us... you an' me. Assuming I ever did travel."

"Can't you have more'n one personal boy?"

"A few gentlemen in New Orleans had 'em a whole entourage... that means a bunch of people in French.... a cook, a valet, a coachman an' footman. But, for me it would look pretentious... like I was puttin' on airs."

"To people with dreary little lives."

Skyler laughed. "You're a real good listener. ...But, tell me if you get an idea that perplexes you."

"'Course I will, so you can educate me." Cartwright was silent a while, gazing up at the lofty ceiling beyond the lamp's gentle glow. Then he said: "I don't rightly know how to say this, Sky, but, sound like you kinda likin' Lucinda for more than just her cookin'."

Skyler sighed. "Yeah, an' that perplexes me, too. ...An' it's somethin' a lot more serious than what people with dreary little lives might think if I had two personal boys."

Cartwright hesitated, then said, "There some massas... I means tho' they married an' gots families... Well, I ain't sho' how to say it."

"I know how to say it," said Skyler. "Though some of 'em call it 'improving their stock.' But, like I already told you, we don't do that at Diligence... 'least according to what I been taught about our family history."

"But, ain't you got every right under God?"

Jess Mowry

"Just 'cause you can do somethin' don't always mean you should." Skyler sighed again. "An' with Lucinda it wouldn't be right. I've... got too much respect for her." He lay a hand on Cartwright's chest. "As a human being like you."

Chapter Fifteen

"Slaves are expensive!" Skyler exclaimed. "Though I'm sure they don't realize that." He pushed the leather-bound ledger away, one of many he'd been reading all morning, and took a sip of lemonade from a tall sweating glass. He sat at his father's mahogany desk, which was piled with papers, bills and receipts, along with stacks of canceled cheques. He was wearing only his new buckskin trousers, which Jupiter's wife had made. Like his old pair, now worn by Cartwright, the fly had laces instead of buttons in the style of an earlier time. She had also worked on Cartwright's because the rear pockets were coming loose. Cartwright had an idea of reinforcing the pockets with rivets -- small copper studs from the harness-maker -- plus adding rivets at other stress points where stitches were likely to break. Cartwright had done this himself -- having once worked in a blacksmith shop -- and Skyler had asked for the same on his trousers.

"Well," said Cartwright patting his belly, which had lost a bit of its stark washboard look. "You could feed us less."

He was comfortably sprawled on a nearby settee, his back to a plush velvet pillow. Although he now had clothes for the house -- blue trousers, white shirts, a red jacket for serving -- he also wore only his leather trousers and sipped a lemonade.

Four days had passed since Skyler's return and, at his father's request, Skyler had spent a lot of that time plowing through ledgers and financial records. Skyler had put on a little more weight from having huge breakfasts of bacon and eggs, sausage and ham, fried potatoes, biscuits, gravy, and hot buttered grits -- food that Betty could cook fairly well -- before spending late mornings reading "the books."

His other duties as heir to the Knights consisted mostly of riding out to watch the slaves at work, reminding them they *were* being watched... along with their watchers, the overseers, who were also slaves but with more privileges, including slightly better cabins a little removed from the Quarters. These men carried whips on their belts, but the whips had only been symbolic for as long a Skyler had been on earth... just to uncoil a whip in the fields required explanation to Skyler's father. The System at Diligence worked very well.

Cartwright always accompanied Skyler, and they rode the enormous Clydesdale. The boys went swimming in the afternoons and hunted in the evenings, taking turns with Skyler's rifle bagging game for the slaves' supper tables and slaying the 'gator that haunted the creek. Nights usually found them in Skyler's room, Skyler reading to Cartwright about King Arthur and his knights; and they'd invented two more different ways. A bit to his mother's dismay -- though her main dismay was the "distressing food" which made a party impossible -- Skyler had darkened to old-penny copper, or rather reverted to it, usually wearing nothing outside but his Indian boots, leather trousers, and savagely-decorated hat.

"It ain't that we feed 'em too much," said Skyler, sipping more lemonade. "They get leavin's from the house... an' for which I pity 'em with the current state of cookin' affairs. An' beans an' rice ain't expensive. An' they got their own little gardens for growin' yams an' such." He pulled his knife from its sheath -- Cartwright had made a new belt for him, being handy with leather -- and sharpened an old-fashioned quill. Then, dipping the tip in a bottle of ink, he made a note in the latest ledger.

"Clothes ain't a big expense either," he added, blotting the note and closing the book. "The field slaves don't wear a lot; cotton shifts for the women an' girls, shorts or trousers for men an' boys, shirts an' coats for wintertime, an' the little ones bare in the summer. 'Course, you gotta dress your house servants well or all the dreary people will talk."

Cartwright laughed. "'Cept for me."

"Even you," said Skyler. "Mother spoke to me yesterday an' insists you dress to serve me at table... though you wouldn't 'offend the food' if you served me wearin' a bone in your nose."

"Why would I wear a bone in my nose?"

"Same reason I'd wear a necktie if you were back in Africa. ...Would you want to go back to Africa?"

"Don't know nobody there, Sky. An' I don't speak African."

Skyler almost said, "but you'd be free," but sheathed the knife instead. "But, Diligence spends a lot on its slaves that other plantations mostly don't. We call a doctor instead of a vet when someone gets sick or hurt. An' a real dentist to tend their teeth... though Jupiter pulls a few now an' then. An' we try to keep the Quarters up an' fit for human beings."

"Thought we was animals, Sky?"

"You know we settled that matter... at least between ourselves... so no teasin' now if you don't mind." Skyler scanned some papers. "Then there's bedding an' household stuff... pots an' pans ain't free. Nor do blankets grow on trees. An' we give 'em candles to use at night 'cause mojo lamps be a hazard of fire."

"At my ol' place we just had a fire. An' the massa wasn't free with wood."

"That makes for gloomy cabins," said Skyler. "An' gloomy cabins make gloomy slaves, which of course affects their work."

"Heard some talk about leakin' roofs."

Skyler frowned. "Yeah, I been hearin' that, too. ...But all those little expenses add up, which eats a big chunk of our profits." He took a last gulp from his glass, then propped his bare feet on the desktop. "Diligence makes a decent profit, but after seein' all these figures I'm starting to think maybe Franklin was right."

"About what?" asked Cartwright.

"...Well... It might be a *little* more efficient to pay a man for his daily work an' then have done with him."

Skyler glanced out the windows, seeing Romulus and Remus cleaning the pond of slimy stuff that might upset his mother. The boys looked cool in the waist-deep water, "accidentally" splashing each other, and Skyler envied them... his father's study was hot and stuffy. "Let your worker take care of himself. Let *him* find a bed to sleep in, an' a roof to put it under. If he gets sick, let him find a doctor. If he needs new clothes or a cookin' pot, let him buy his own. An' if he mistreats his wife an' kids, why should I have to intervene? ...That means get involved an' correct him."

"Sound like what you told Jimmy 'bout how things be in the North."

"...Well... yes it does. ...But I ain't no greedy factory owner."

Cartwright sipped more lemonade. "Does sound like a lot of trouble, takin' care of us."

Skyler sighed. "Next I'll be sittin' up like my father, pondering over my problems at night. Most of which are caused by my slaves. '...Little Willie has a fever. Remus cut his toe. Dorry an' Joseph been fightin' again.' ...An' I won't even mention the breedin' problems, 'specially when you got randy young bucks."

Cartwright laughed. "Like you an' me?"

"Please, no teasin' now," said Skyler. "It's a serious matter, Cartwright, choosin' who's gonna mate with whom to breed for strength an' docility... that means gentleness an' submitting to your master."

"Like our horse?" asked Cartwright.

"Exactly. You want a strong yet gentle beast who's also fairly smart."

"But not smart enough to get ideas?"

Skyler flipped a pencil at Cartwright. "Maybe it's best if I don't buy Lucky... even assuming I could."

Cartwright laughed again. "Ain't like him an' me could breed."

"You'd probably breed a bunch of ideas."

"You an' me been breedin' some."

"But nobody else is gonna know 'em, so they ain't gonna multiply."

"But, if you don't buy Lucky, don't that mean...?"

"Means I can't buy Lucinda," sighed Skyler. "But I don't want to dwell on that now."

Cartwright held up a catalogue that had come by post the day before. He'd been looking through the illustrations. "Look at this, Sky. It sorta like a railroad engine, 'cept it run free with no tracks. It can pull three plows at a time. Or a reaper like our horse. It can power a buzz saw, too. An' do lots of other useful stuff."

"How you know all that?" asked Skyler.

"Show it here in these pictures."

Skyler came over to study the book. "That thing cost nearly a thousand dollars!"

"But it do the work of twenty slaves an' it don't eat nothin' but water an' wood. It don't get sick or cut its toe. Or get no ideas."

Skyler shrugged. "I don't know much about steam engines. But I know they break down sometimes. Then you have to get a mechanic, who probably costs more than a doctor."

"I knows a bit about 'em," said Cartwright. "When they rented me out to the railroad I helped with some work on the engine. The engineer say I gots appetite for runnin' an' fixin' mechanical things."

"Aptitude," said Skyler.

"Aptitude," echoed Cartwright, committing the word to memory.

Skyler shrugged again. "Father ain't much on new ideas. Only reason he bought the reaper was Little Miss Chicken Feet's daddy got one."

"Somebody gots to be first to try out new ideas."

Skyler frowned. "Being first can be dangerous. 'Specially with new ideas. May we change the subject, please?"

"Been a while since breakfast."

Skyler glanced at a long clock. "I'm a bit hungry myself, but it's still a couple hours till lunch. Maybe we can go swimming after... if father don't want me to ride out again an' watch more slaves at work."

Cartwright relaxed on the pillow. "S'pose you could ring for some more lemonade?"

"That ain't a bad idea."

Skyler reached for a velvet rope, but the butler appeared in the doorway, looking more than a little perplexed. "Pardon me, Masta Knight, but that *boy* of Masta Franklin's is here. At the *front* door! He said he has a letter for you, but insists it's only for your hand."

"Well, show him in, Jacob."

"Yes, suh." The butler turned to go, but Danny appeared in the doorway, panting, sweaty, and muddied with dust in only trousers and battered blue cap. He had to lean backward to balance his belly; and how he kept his trousers on -- if it could be said they were actually on -- was a mystery worthy of Auguste Dupin. Their cuffs completely concealed his feet, and had left a trail of dust behind on the mirror polished hallway floor.

"Mornin', Massa Knight. Brung y'all a letter."

Skyler smiled. "C'mon in, Danny." He glanced at the glowering butler. "Thank you, Jacob. Would you send in a pitcher of lemonade, please?"

"I rather have a beer," said Danny. "An' it been a while since breakfast."

Skyler laughed. "All of three hours by your time. How 'bout a sandwich to hold you till lunch?"

"How 'bout two of 'em?" said Danny. "Roast beef an' mustard. I gots to ride back with your answer, an' ridin' is hungry-makin' work."

"All right," said Skyler. "An' I'll give you a note to Tom at the tavern. You can have lunch there on your way back."

"An' tell him I needs help back on my horse."

Skyler glanced at the butler again, whose eyebrows threatened to fly into space. "Please see to the sandwiches, Jacob."

"Yes, suh."

"An' the beer," added Danny, waddling in. He plopped his rolly bulk on a chair, which made a tortured sound.

"Danny," said Skyler, "This is my companion Cartwright. Cartwright, this is Danny, Lucky's little brother."

Danny grinned at Cartwright. "Well, ain't you lucky!" He extracted a sweat-sodden envelope from somewhere under his blubber. Skyler took it as a maid came in with a pitcher of beer and a trio of mugs on a silver tray. She stared astonished at Danny.

"Thank you, Deborah," said Skyler. "Set it on the table, please. Cartwright will serve."

The maid gave Cartwright a doubtful look as if she thought he would break everything, but set down the tray and left the room with another astonished appraisal of Danny.

The envelope was sealed with wax, but there was no signet.

Block letters said:

SIR SKYLER KNIGHT.
TO BE DELIVERED INTO HIS OWN HAND.

Skyler smiled. "Since when did I become a knight?"

"Huh?" asked Cartwright, pouring the beer.

"It's a joke," said Skyler. "'Sir Knight.'"

"Oh, like you been readin' to me. When knights was knighted sirs by the king, an' they had to earn the right to be sirs by doin' somethin' noble."

"Which I haven't," said Skyler, opening the envelope. "But these aren't the days of chivalry when there were noble things to do." He unfolded the letter:

My Dear Sir Knight: (it read)

I beg you will do me the Honour of dining with me this evening. Shall we say about seven o'clock?

Your humble Servant.

Loki (Esq.)

"Well, I be dammed!" said Skyler. "I got a dinner invite from a slave!"

Cartwright laughed. "'Spect that a new idea!"

Chapter Sixteen

"**S**kyler, are you free?" his mother called from out in the hall.

"Yes, mother."

Skyler's mother swept into the room, her dress a profusion of bows and lace, her ruffled skirts skimming the floor as if she was wearing a huge bluebell flower below her narrow waist. If Franklin moved like a full-rigged ship majestically tacking into the wind, Skyler's mother was a graceful sloop responding to the slightest breeze. But halfway across the room she stopped as if the breeze had suddenly failed.

"Good heavens!" she cried, spying Danny. "What is this half-clothed girl doing here?" She seemed to be in conflict as whether to avert her eyes or allow them to openly stare. "Surely she isn't one of ours?"

Skyler laughed. "He's a he, mother, and he's Franklin's. He brought me a letter."

Danny struggled out of the chair and doffed his cap with a courtly bow. "At your service, ma'am."

Skyler's mother recovered her poise and came sweeping up to Danny. Her delicate nostrils quivered a bit -- Danny smelled very much like a boy, and there was a lot of him to smell -- but she graciously patted his head. "He certainly has nice manners, though I've never seen a child so... large. Franklin surely feeds him well! How old do you think he is?"

"Twelve, I believe," said Skyler.

"My goodness! ...You received a letter from Seth Franklin? What-ever about, if I may ask?"

"Just some... business... at Content."

"I'm sure your father will be pleased at your taking an interest in business. In fact, he spoke with me this morning just along those lines. He wishes me to consult with you on matters regarding the servants. No doubt he intends it as practice."

"...Oh," said Skyler, glancing at Cartwright, who stood politely with lowered eyes by the pitcher of beer on the table.

Cartwright prompted softly, "Y'all wanna dismiss us, suh?"

"No," said Skyler. "You an' Danny sit down over there an' have your refreshment. ...Unless you wish privacy, mother?"

"Thank you, Skyler, but it may be well if Carter hears this."

"His name is Cartwright, mother."

"Of course. It concerns the lawn boys... Ronald and, er..."

"Romulus and Remus, mother."

"Of course. Well, yesterday I saw one of them with a peacock feather! Of course I was very upset!"

Skyler glanced at Cartwright and Danny, who had taken their mugs to a settee. "Of course you were, mother."

"He *claimed* he'd found it on the lawn, but I'm *sure* he pulled it out of a bird!"

"...Um, yeah, that's where feathers mostly come from." Skyler glanced at the boys again: Cartwright looked properly solemn, but Danny was openly grinning.

Skyler's mother went on, "Of course I took it away from him... I have it right here." She searched among her ruffles. "And of course I gave the boy a scolding."

"Of course," said Skyler, regarding the rainbowy feather in his mother's delicate hand. "But I don't think I can glue it back on."

"Beggin' your pardons," said Cartwright, coming over submissively. "Them feathers be like a new fashion in France among the noble ladies, ma'am. They wears 'em on they hats."

"Indeed?" said Skyler's mother.

"Yes, ma'am." Cartwright picked up a catalogue. "Here a noble lady wearin' one."

"How nice!" exclaimed Skyler's mother. "And I have just the hat!" She patted Cartwright's head. "What an intelligent boy!"

"So I've noticed," said Skyler.

The maid came in with two sandwiches on another silver tray, and Skyler inclined his head toward Danny.

But then his mother's face fell. "I just don't know what to *do*, Skyler, about your homecoming party, when Betty can only produce such... roughage."

"Beggin' your pardon," said Cartwright again. "But maybe y'all could have a party kinda special to somethin'?"

Skyler's mother cocked her head. "Special to something?"

Skyler raised an eyebrow at Cartwright. "I believe he means a theme."

"Indeed? And what would be the theme?"

"Well, ma'am," said Cartwright. "We is out here in the bayou, an' Betty can cook bayou food real good. An' massa Skyler do be a kind of bayou boy. ...I means in a noble way, a'course." He patted Skyler's head. "Don't he look noble right now, ma'am? Just like a knight come back from a quest all rough 'n tumble an' sorta such. An' he slay that 'gator, which be a kind of dragon, so that make him even more noble."

"Of course!" exclaimed Skyler's mother. "I can picture it quite well! We would have red and white chequered cloths. And common lanterns on the tables. And the servants dressed as bayou folk. What a grand idea!" She gave Skyler's chubby cheek a pinch. "So perfect for my wild cherub!"

Skyler scowled at Cartwright. "Positively meteoric."

"Carter is such an intelligent boy!"

"He is quick on the uptake," growled Skyler.

"I must start planning!" Grabbing up her skirts, Skyler's mother swept out of the room, but paused in the hall to look back. "You will punish Randolf for pulling the feather?"

Skyler sighed. "Of course, mother." Then he scowled at Cartwright again. "That was a bad idea!"

"'Spect I gots a whippin' comin'?"

"Oh, shut up."

Danny had finished the first sandwich and was halfway through the second. "Don't you like parties? I sho' does."

"I wish you could take my place at this one! ...Bunch of dreary boring people! Pretentious, pompous, posturing... peacocks! Not to mention Miss Chicken Feet!" Skyler faced Cartwright again. "Why did you have to open your trap an' give mother that idea?"

"Well, Sky, seem she kinda lonely sometimes, livin' out here with nothin' to do 'cept worry 'bout feathers gettin' yanked."

Skyler snorted. "I been tempted to yank a few myself! Nasty ol' birds that screech all night an' sneak up an' peck your behind! Don't have no purpose 'cept flauntin' their tails an' showin' off to each other! Bet they don't even taste good!"

Cartwright went on, "Your mother been wantin' that party, Sky. Seem like you make her happy 'least you pretend to like it."

"...I never thought about it that way."

"Does you gots to kiss Miss Chicken Feet?"

Skyler stuck a finger down his throat, put out his tongue and crossed his eyes.

"Who gots chicken feet?" asked Danny.

"Never you mind," said Skyler.

Cartwright spread his hands. "Then why it be so bad, Sky? I means if you makin' your mother happy? I seen you face that big ol' 'gator with just that one shot in your gun. An' stand up to Jimmy when he had a knife. Why a little ol' party perplex you?"

Skyler sighed. "You haven't been to one."

Danny finished his second sandwich and washed it down with beer. "I don't think you gonna be perplexed at Lucky's party tonight!"

Chapter Seventeen

"**Y**ou can have your own horse, you know?" Skyler ducked his head, Cartwright doing the same, as the titanic horse ambled under a tree and streamers of moss slithered over their backs.

"I's not used to doin' things by myself," said Cartwright, flicking some moss off his shoulder. "All my life I been told what to do... when to get up an' when to eat, what to work at an' when to sleep. I still gets confused when you gives me a choice or ask if I wanna do somethin'."

"You managed some things on your own," said Skyler. "An' you got life education."

"But most things be better with you, Sky. Like ridin' with you, an' talkin' 'bout stuff. An' huntin' an' fishin' an' swimmin'." Cartwright smiled. "An' learnin' different ways."

"An' breedin' ideas?"

"Two does breed 'em better than one."

Skyler was riding behind Cartwright while Cartwright tended the reins. The boys were shirtless as usual and still in their buckskin trousers. Cartwright was naturally barefoot, while Skyler wore his Indian boots along with his knife and feathered hat. Their evening clothes were rolled in a blanket that lay across the horse's shoulders, along with Skyler's rifle. The boys had eaten a massive lunch of "dirty rice" and crawfish pie – two of Betty's *tour de forces* -- and the ample food combined with the heat had made them drowse as they rode. Fortunately the dangling moss warned them in time to duck low branches.

The huge horse clopped down the tree-shaded road through occasional patches of leaf-dappled sun, seeming to enjoy the idea of simply going for a walk. Cartwright asked, "S'pose there be time for a beer in town?"

"Franklin's got the best beer in the world. An' the food is meteoric!" Skyler glanced at the sun through the leaves. "But we got time for a beer at the tavern, an' I have mine out back with you."

"Ain't folks gonna talk?"

"Some folks always talk. An' the ones who have the least to say are the ones who usually talk the most."

"Thought any more about buyin' them twins?"

"I brought my cheque book along. But remember it was Lucky's idea, an' Franklin might not think it's good."

Cartwright tapped the horse with his heels as it suddenly came to a stop. Its tall ears tilted forward as if it had heard a sound ahead, but then it slowly moved on.

Then, they heard the crack of a whip. The horse came to another halt as the snap of leather sounded again. This time there was a cry of pain.

Cartwright clutched the reins as the horse showed the whites of its gentle brown eyes.

"Go on," said Skyler, as the whip cracked again, bringing another cry. The horse shied back and tried to retreat.

Cartwright steadied the uneasy beast, then gently urged him forward. Another whiplash cut the air as they rounded a bend in the road. A black boy was down on his knees in the dirt. He looked about eight and was thin as a rail; nothing between his skin and bones but small kid-muscles and maybe a prayer. He was gleaming with sweat and naked... except for a huge canvas pack on his back and a big iron collar around his slim neck. A short length of rope was tied to the collar and gripped by a lean white man, whose tattered clothes and greasy hat proclaimed his social status. He seemed to be around thirty, though his sunburned face was deeply lined. His other hand held a cat-'o-nine-tails, and he cocked his arm for another lash at the cowering boy on the ground.

"Please!" cried the boy, struggling to rise but clearly exhausted:

the pack was so enormous it should have been on a mule. "I can't, suh!"

Skyler gripped Cartwright's shoulders, rose up behind him and yelled, "Stop that!"

The man hesitated, obviously wanting to whip the boy but startled by the gigantic horse. He dropped the rope and edged away as the massive animal came to a halt. He eyed the half-naked boys on its back, obviously noting their primitive trousers, along with Skyler's savage hat, shoulder-length-hair and Indian boots. His lips drew back from long yellow teeth.

"An' who might you be givin' me orders?"

Skyler scowled down at the man. "You'd best add sir when speaking to me."

The young boy stayed on his knees in the dirt, though he raised his eyes to the mammoth horse as if he was seeing a vision. The man pulled out a half-empty bottle, took a gulp and laughed.

"Be a cold day in hell when I say 'suh' to a half-breed buck like you. ...Boy!"

Cartwright was looking uncertain -- after all the man was white -- but Skyler slid to the ground. "Mind the horse, Cartwright. I don't want him stepping on trash and getting his hooves defiled."

The man spit in the dust at Skyler's feet. The young boy covered his head with his arms as the man cocked the whip and readied to swing, but Skyler stepped between them and grabbed a handful of lashes.

"My name is Skyler Knight. You're obviously not from around here, but you might have heard that name." He nodded down the road. "In the town of Knight's Crossing."

The man tensed a little at this, and his whip hand fell to his side. Several expressions crossed his face, but he finally settled for halfway civil. "Sorry, suh," he gruffed. "But you gotta admit you sho' ain't dressed like a young gentleman."

"If you could read," said Skyler. "You'd know you can't judge a book by its cover." He glanced at the cowering boy. "Take off that pack."

"Y'all wait a minute!" cried the man. "You got no right..."

"I got *every* right!" snarled Skyler, flinging away the lashes. He glanced again at the small thin boy, who seemed afraid to obey him. "Take it off, son," Skyler said gently.

"I can't, suh! After you gone he whip me worse!"

"You're under my protection now. You belong to this... person?"

The ragged man glared. "'Course he..."

"Shut up!" roared Skyler. "When I want to hear something out of your mouth, I'll ask you a god-dammed question!"

"He gots a gun!" yelled the boy.

"I saw it," said Skyler, facing the man, whose hand had gone into his coat. "Silly ol' pinfire relic."

There was an ominous triple-click sound. The man spun around, looking into the bore of the .50 caliber Smith. "Your nigger's aimin' at a white man!"

Skyler smiled. "Remember he's only an animal. He's *fairly* well trained, but of course you know how animals are, and I can't be sure what he might do if you should startle him." He turned again to the boy. "I asked if you belong to this... person?"

The boy was looking more scared than ever. "Not a'zactly, suh."

"What do you mean?"

The man thrust a hand back into his coat. Cartwright's finger tensed on the trigger, but the man pulled out a folded paper and shoved it into Skyler's hands. Then he tore the pack off the boy and jerked him to his feet by the collar so Skyler could see the two ugly scars burned across his slender back. One was an owner's brand, the other a damming **Я**. There were also many stripes, and more than a few were fresh.

"This be his *second* run... suh," said the man.

Skyler unfolded the grimy poster, which pictured a hand-drawn likeness and described the boy and his brands.

"Any more questions? ...Suh?" The man glared up at Cartwright. "I see how you treat your niggers 'round here... pampered pets look like to me! But *this* boy belong in Mississippi. As you can see from that poster. ...Suh."

Skyler glanced at Cartwright, whose eyes were narrowed behind the gun sights, then faced the ragged man again. "The reward is fifty dollars. I'll pay you that right now."

He nodded to Cartwright. "Toss me down my cheque book, please." He turned to the man again. "The bank in town will cash it, as will any other bank for fifty miles around. And this will be more convenient for you than having to take the boy... home. Assuming he lives to complete the journey." Skyler held out the poster. "I trust you know this says, *alive?*"

The man looked uncertain now, scanning Skyler again... the crude leather trousers, the coppery tan, the battered old hat with its feral adornments. "But, the boy ain't yours, suh. ...Beggin' your pardon."

"His owner's address is on the poster; I'll send him a telegram," said Skyler. "You needn't trouble yourself anymore, and you'll have your money today, instead of..." He scanned the poster again. "having to wait another week." He studied the exhausted boy. "And I doubt he would live that long."

The man considered. "It's twenty-five dollars just for his skin."

"Would you rather have fifty dollars now, or twenty-five next week? And have to bother skinning him?"

"I'd be a fool not to take your fifty. Boy's already 'bout half dead."

"So I've noticed," said Skyler.

"Here, massa," said Cartwright, tossing the cheque book to Skyler.

Skyler frowned. "Dammit, I don't have a pen."

Cartwright slid down from the horse. "Let me have your knife, suh."

"Huh?"

Cartwright drew Skyler's blade from its sheath and cut the back of his hand. "'Spect this do as ink, suh?"

"Is that legal?" asked the man. "Writin' a cheque in nigger blood?"

"Of course," said Skyler. "And, perhaps in this case, appropriate." He snapped a twig from a nearby bush, took back his knife, sharpened the twig, then dipped the tip in Cartwright's blood. Cartwright turned around so Skyler could write the cheque on his back.

"Your name?" asked Skyler. "And remove the boy's collar."

"Had it riveted on, suh. ...Cost me two dollars."

"I'll add it to the amount," said Skyler.

The man regarded the mammoth horse. "I'd take it as a favor, suh, if you could take my pack to town an' leave it at the tavern?"

"I take it as an insult," said Skyler, "that you even ask." He smiled at the boy, who was gazing at him in wide-eyed wonder. "We'll get that dammed thing off your neck as soon as we get to town."

Chapter Eighteen

"You gonna send him back?" asked Cartwright.

The huge horse clopped at its leisurely pace nearing the outskirts of Knight's Crossing where cabins were scattered among the trees. They had left the man muttering curses while struggling into his monstrous pack, and the boy now nestled between Skyler and Cartwright. He'd said his name was Andrew, and he'd burst into tears as Skyler untied the rope from his collar. Skyler and Cartwright had soothed the boy, who was not only scared, beaten and starved but had never been on a horse before. Andrew had cried for a while but then, exhausted, had fallen asleep.

"'Course not," said Skyler, his arms around the boy's thin body cradling him to his chest. "But I don't know what to do with him. I never thought any farther ahead than getting' him away from that... *thing*... that passes itself for a human being." He regarded Andrew. "He can't be worth much anymore, 'specially runnin' away twice."

Cartwright ducked a low-hanging branch. "He be worth even less if you send him back. You know what his massa do to him."

"He'd be used as a warning to other slaves, just like nailin' up his skin if he'd died at the hands of that... *thing*. But he'd be killed anyhow, an' hung in a tree for the crows to pick, after they whipped the skin off his bones."

Cartwright was silent a minute or two, tending the reins as they came into town, which was mostly deserted at this time of day with the sun like a blazing brass ball overhead. There were only a few figures in sight and all of them were black... a man repairing a wooden sidewalk, a woman sweeping the general store porch, and a sweating boy at the blacksmith shop shoveling coal from a wagon. All paused their work for a moment to gaze at the enormous horse and its three outlandish riders. Finally, Cartwright asked, "You gonna send that telegram?"

"I have to do something," said Skyler. "I can't be lettin' slaves run away; it gives other slaves ideas. An' it's worse if they think he *got* away 'cause then they think it's possible."

"*Is* it possible, Sky?"

"...Well... just about anything's possible if one is brave and determined. ...Might even be easier now with all that Abolition stuff. They been sendin' down agitators to give slaves bad ideas... like what happened to Jimmy. An' they got an underground railroad to help slaves run away."

Cartwright cocked his head. "Mean a train that run underground? Like in a tunnel up to the North?"

"It's a figure of speech," said Skyler. "It's not an actual railroad, just people who hide runaways by day an' guide 'em North at night." He hesitated a moment. "Some of 'em white, from what I hear. ...But don't you tell *no* one I said that."

"Thank you, Sky," said Cartwright.

"For what?"

"For tellin' me the truth."

"It just slipped out 'cause I'm sleepy an' stupid."

"Now you ain't tellin' the truth."

Skyler looked down at Andrew, making sure he was still asleep. "It's probably somethin' you *should* know. I'm gonna give you a horse, an' a paper sayin' you got the right to ride around on your own. An' if I wanted to travel some day... however unlikely that seems... if I took you anywhere out of the South... say, up North or to some other country... you wouldn't be a slave anymore."

"Mean I could quit my job of bein' your companion?"

"If you wanted to. ...Um, think you would?"

Cartwright thought for a while as the horse ambled through the little town, drawing many curious looks from mostly brown or ebony eyes. Finally he looked back and smiled. "You'd have to be a lot meaner to me than what you been so far."

"Have I been mean to you?"

"It just a figure of speech."

Skyler glanced at Andrew again. "Maybe we should change the subject."

Cartwright nodded. "He ob'visly got some bad ideas."

"Well, I'm tryin' to think of a good one for him, but I haven't got much to work with."

They arrived at the railroad station, and Skyler slid off to the platform. Andrew stirred but didn't wake up. Two sweating slaves, big brawny men, were loading a heavy freight wagon. Both paused to regard the mammoth horse, then saw Andrew's back. "We's workin' hard, suh," said one.

"I can see that," said Skyler... though he hadn't noticed and found he didn't care.

He went into the station and was gone a few minutes. Then he returned and remounted the horse by climbing the wagon's rear wheel. Andrew woke up and stared around, his big-eyed face showing new fear, but Skyler smiled and patted his head.

"You're dead, Andrew."

The boy burst into tears. "No! Please!"

"...That's not what I meant. I sent a telegram to your master; told him I shot you for stealin' a chicken, an' I ain't gonna bother to send him your skin so he don't owe me nothin'.."

Cartwright frowned. "You coulda said that better, Sky!"

"Sorry," said Skyler. "You hungry, Andrew?"

The boy wiped his face. "Sho' is, suh." Then he hugged Skyler tight. "Thank you, massa! I never run away from you!"

"You better not," said Skyler. "You'll carry that brand for the rest of your life an' everybody will know what you are." He looked over Andrew's head at Cartwright. "Father won't be pleased about this: we've never had a runaway, an' he'd never buy a branded boy."

"Maybe he could work in the house an' wear a shirt all the time?"

"You know better than that," said Skyler. "Won't be a day before our slaves know everything about him. An' I sure as hell can't treat him nice. I have to give him the dirtiest, lowest, nastiest work."

"I don't care!" cried Andrew. "I does anythin' you say for gettin' me away from that man!" Tears rolled down his cheeks again. "He use me like girl, suh! 'Cept I don't got girl parts."

Skyler glared back up the road. "I should go back an' shoot that... *thing!* Then drag it into the bayou an' let the 'gators eat it!"

"I helps you, suh!" said Andrew.

Skyler looked into the little boy's eyes. "Listen, Andrew... an' this is the truth. Ain't nobody can change the past no matter how bad it was. You probably won't forget what happened, but you can't let it make you hate, 'cause that will only hurt you more."

Cartwright nodded. "He right, Andrew, that the truth."

Skyer patted Andrew's shoulder. "I'll think of something to do with you, an' I'll make it as good as I can. Right now let's get you something to eat. ...Ow! That collar is hot in the sun! I wish it was at the devil! We better go to the blacksmith first an' have the dammed thing off."

"I's awful hungry, massa," said Andrew.

"My name is Skyler... when we're alone."

"I understands... Skyler."

Cartwright said, "Franklin's blacksmith could take it off."

"That's a good idea," said Skyler. "Then nobody can talk."

They rode back to town, and then around to the rear of the tavern. There stood a hugely fat horse cropping grass. And there was Danny sprawled in the shade, his cap pulled over his face. An empty platter and pitcher beside him explained the reason why. Andrew stared. "Lord, that boy is fat!"

Skyler smiled. "Also somewhat in my displeasure."

Andrew looked scared again. "You gonna whip him?"

"Hush," said Cartwright gently. "You ain't in Mississippi no more."

Skyler slid off and knelt beside Danny to shake his shoulder. Danny yawned and lifted his cap. "...Oh. Afternoon, Massa Knight."

"*Late* afternoon," said Skyler. "You should have been home by now an' let Lucky know we were comin'."

Danny yawned again. "Guess I ate a little too much." He burped. "'Scuse me. Reckon I best be on my way, if y'all help me up on my horse."

"Oh, never mind," said Skyler. "You wouldn't get there before we did... not on that horse. Lucky will probably assume we're coming." He turned to Cartwright. "I'll get us some food an' beer."

Danny studied Andrew as Cartwright helped him down off the horse. "Why you be so skinny? An' wearin' that nasty collar?"

"He from Mississippi," said Cartwright.

Danny frowned. "I heard about that place!" Then he pillowed his head on his arms. "I could do with another beer, Sky."

Andrew whistled. "Now I *knows* I ain't in 'sippi!"

Chapter Nineteen

T he sun was lowering over the swamp as the huge horse ambled into Content beneath the wooden gateway. The journey from town had been slow because Danny's mount only waddled along, puffing like a locomotive and stopping often to eat more grass. Skyler was at the reins of his steed, though he'd been dozing for most of the way, and Andrew was sleeping behind him secure in Cartwright's arms. The boy had eaten everything Skyler had brought him at the tavern, gobbling it down like a dog who'd been starved, and his tummy stuck out so round and tight it looked like he'd swallowed a cannon ball. Cartwright was also half asleep, and Danny was dozing peacefully upon his horse's acre of back.

Skyler leading, they came up the drive through the green cane fields, where Franklin's slaves worked at their unhurried pace; and everyone paused as Skyler passed to wave or call a greeting as if they'd all invited him. Skyler smiled and nodded back, despite it being very strange... good slaves kept their eyes on the ground and never greeted visitors. He'd ridden through many such fields in his life, full of silent, sweating people who hacked and chopped with long sharp blades. His only protection had been his skin and all the power it symbolized, not his single-shot rifle. His father had taught him to see everything in a single sweeping glance, and had warned him never to look back because it was a sign of fear. But, all these smiles unsettled him, and he often glanced over his shoulder, surprised to see that faces still smiled after his shadow had passed.

Halfway to the house was a big oak tree, and he halted the horse in its shade. Cartwright woke up and looked around.

"Guess we's here," he said, stretching and yawning, which didn't wake Andrew.

"We best put on our shirts," said Skyler. "To make our arrival proper."

"Ain't no need to be formal," said Danny, also waking and sitting up as his puffing horse drew even with Skyler's. "It Lucky who invited you."

"I've been wondering if that was a joke... Franklin havin' a little fun."

"Nope, it be Lucky's party sho' nuff."

Cartwright laughed. "'Spect even the nigger food be good here, from what I seen of you an' your brother." He sniffed the air. "An' it do smell... what that word, Sky?"

"Meteoric," said Skyler, and it certainly did. He wondered if Lucinda had cooked.

Andrew woke up. "I smells food!"

"Reckon you'll get your share," said Skyler.

Danny nudged his horse with his heels and the blubbery beast almost trotted. "His supper waitin', too!" Danny laughed.

The sun was turning ruddy-gold as it touched the tops of cypress trees. The field slaves were ceasing their work, most climbing aboard a pair of wagons loaded with bundles of fragrant cane. Skyler studied them again, looking for details he might have missed but only being mystified. He saw no overseers, yet some people lingered to finish a job, completing a bundle or loading a wagon as if they actually cared. And all kept their long gleaming blades: again there weren't any overseers to collect and count those potential weapons. Slave uprisings were historically rare, and the details usually kept suppressed lest other slaves get ideas; though Skyler had heard of masters and families hacked to pieces by -- he assumed -- badly mistreated slaves. These slaves looked far from mistreated; still, it seemed as if Franklin was careless.

As when he'd arrived the week before, he was met at the house by a crowd of kids who seemed to have nothing to do but play. Compared to their chubby and well-filled forms, Andrew looked almost skeletal despite his bulging tummy. The children stared at his collar as if they had never seen such a thing. Cartwright dismounted to help Andrew down, and the children's eyes widened seeing his back. Laughter died and smiles disappeared.

"Why you wearin' that?" asked a girl.

"Who whip you like that?" asked a boy.

"He been branded, too!" cried another.

"Y'all hush up," said an older girl. "He don't need remindin' what bad been done."

Skyler expected accusing looks, but none of the kids seemed to think he'd done it.

"Andrew," called Danny, still on his horse. "Y'all come with me. We get you washed up an' somethin' to wear. Then I take that damn thing off." He prodded his chest balloons with a thumb. "I also be the blacksmith boy."

Skyler dismounted and handed his horse's reins to Andrew. "Think you can handle him? He's mighty big an' strong."

"Biggest horse in the world," added Cartwright.

Andrew puffed his slender chest. "Sho' I can! ...C'mon, big beast!" He tugged on the reins and the huge horse followed. The rest of the children tagged along, though staying well clear of those barrel-sized hooves.

Skyler was eager to see Lucinda -- and whether or not that was proper -- so he was disappointed when Lucky opened the door. Lucky was "dressed" in cotton shorts that couldn't be seen in a full frontal view.

"Welcome, Sir Knight," said Lucky, grinning at Skyler, who'd doffed his hat hoping for Lucinda. "Ain't no need to be formal."

"Um," said Skyler, quickly clamping on his hat, then drawing Cartwright forward. "This is Cartwright. My father bought him for me. You remember meetin' him at the station?"

Lucky looked thoughtful at this, but smiled at Cartwright and offered a hand. "A pleasure to see you again, sir. You're lookin' quite prosperous now."

Cartwright seemed a little confused. "Um... my new massa treat me nice."

Lucky laughed. "'Course he does, though he don't know why.

But hopefully he'll figure it out." Then he lumbered aside. "Won't you step in, gentlemen."

"Um?" asked Cartwright. "Both of us?"

"I don't see no other gentlemen, sir." Lucky led the way up the hall, displaying the massive black moons of his bottom, though Skyler regarded the paintings that hung along the walls. As when he'd been here previously, he thought them all quite good.

Arriving in Franklin's library where lamps had already been lit, Lucky asked, "Would you like some refreshment, sirs? A julep, rum punch... or maybe a beer?"

Skyler was finding this all very strange, as if they had crossed into some other land by passing the gates of Content. "Um, is your master at home?"

"He's fishin' at the moment, sir. A disciple of Izaak Walton."

"Um, yes," said Skyler. "I've read a bit of Walton's work."

Lucky smiled. "Reading can be so enlightening. I expect Master Franklin will return soon, though he generally takes a nap at that time, bein' an early riser, an' won't be joinin' us for dinner, havin' some letters to write. But, I'm sure he'd be delighted if you wish to speak with him."

"Um, no," said Skyler. "I wouldn't want to disturb him."

"Y'all want a beer or not?"

"Yes, please. And thank you," said Skyler, feeling stranger with each passing minute.

"Make yourselves at home, gentlemen." Lucky pointed to a table. "There's today's New Orleans paper come on the mornin' train, if you wish to peruse the news. We live in such enlightened times. Next there'll be a telegraph in everybody's house." He bowed, which wasn't easy for him, then waddled out of the room.

Skyler glanced at Cartwright. "This is rather unusual."

Cartwright shrugged. "I don't know what usual, Sky. Just reckon this house run different from yours."

"It's different all right!" said Skyler, picking up the paper. "But, I hope you don't think this is normal! ...Near-naked slave boys answering doors an' play-acting gentleman talk!"

Cartwright bowed. "I thought it was simply good manners, sir."

Skyler frowned. "Don't you start! ...Reminds me of a story by Edgar Allan Poe. About a new system. ...'Cept it was in a madhouse."

"Think there gonna be telegraphs in everybody's house someday?"

"I don't know," said Skyler. "But we'd all have to learn the Morse Code."

Cartwright studied the leather-bound books filling the shelves around the room. "So, you can read all these, Sky? Or does you call it perusin'?"

"Perusing," said Skyler, "is different from readin'... kinda not payin' as much attention as when you're really readin'."

"Guess I ain't allowed to peruse neither?"

"I'm gonna teach you readin'. But..."

"I won't say nothin' to nobody." Cartwright looked around again. "I like them pretty pictures. They's even black people in some of 'em."

"They're really quite good, I think... Damn it to hell!" Skyler flung the paper away.

"Peruse somethin' nasty?" asked Cartwright.

"God-dammed Abolitionists! They're gonna keep stirrin' up trouble until..." He pictured Franklin's slaves, all apparently happy, but with deadly weapons. "...Well, I don't know what. But I wish they were all at the devil!"

"...Oh," said Cartwright, then pointed. "Look, Sky! There be a sword like in your knight books."

Skyler turned to the polished blade shining in the lamplight. "Yeah, that's somethin', ain't it? Belonged to Franklin's ancestor who was a real knight."

The boys went over to look at the sword, and Cartwright asked, "How come you don't buy one for yourself?"

"'Cause it would just *be* somethin' I bought. I wouldn't be... well, entitled to it."

"But, didn't your ancestors used to be knights?"

Skyler laughed. "My ancestors used to make wagons. Guess you could say we were cart wrights. We were never nobility until we came here an' invented our own by play-actin' ways we read of in books."

"But, *you* woulda risen in them days, Sky. Done somethin' noble an' been made a knight."

"I'm sure you would have been a knight, too. A noble blacka-moor knight."

"Maybe we woulda gone questin' together."

"Maybe we did," said Skyler. "There's a theory about things like that; people meetin' in future times who met in times before."

"I've also read that theory, and perhaps all three of us met be-fore."

Skyler and Cartwright turned around as Lucky came in with three mugs on a tray. Lucky saw the crumpled paper. "Read anything up-settin', sir?"

"No," said Skyler.

Skyler and Cartwright each took mugs, and Lucky set the tray on a table. "I'll show y'all to your room in a bit so you can freshen up for supper." He glanced at the Ormolu clock. "Which will be served at eight." He smiled again at the shirtless boys. "Formal dress is not required. In fact, I don't recommend it. It's rather warm for super-fluous clothes, wouldn't you agree?"

Skyler shrugged. "When in Rome..."

"Exactly, suh." Lucky picked up and refolded the paper. "I see you have some color now, and may I say it suits you."

Skyler frowned. "My color don't make any difference to anyone but a fool."

"I quite agree, sir," said Lucky. "Intelligence comes in every color, along with compassion, kindness and love. As, unfortunately, does cruelty, ignorance and hate. ...Of course you'll be stayin' the night. The ride through the swamp can be so dreary after the sun goes down. And you might wish to see Master Franklin tomorrow... per-haps to discuss a purchase?"

"I might," said Skyler. "If a certain sassy someone don't make it seem like a bad idea."

"It's only fair to let you know what you might be buyin', sir. ...Both ends of the horse, so to speak."

"I've already seen the end that eats, an' more than a bit of the other."

"*Touché*, Sir Knight." Lucky took the third mug, then plopped down in Franklin's huge chair. "Pray be seated, gentlemen." He took a sip of beer. "What have you been doin', Sir Knight? Slay any dragons? Right any wrongs?"

Chapter Twenty

"**I** sees what you sayin'," said Cartwright. "Things does seem a little strange around here."

"More than a little," said Skyler. "Like somethin' written by Jonathan Swift!"

It was just after seven o'clock. The boys had been "shown" to their second-floor room -- Lucky declining to climb the stairs -- and Cartwright was filling a basin in preparation to wash. "Wanna go first?" he asked, setting the pitcher back on the washstand.

"After you," said Skyler, who'd been wondering where Lucinda might be. Logically, she was probably cooking, something she obviously did very well, but he wondered if she liked to cook.

He stood at the window watching the sunset, the sky turning rose and gold in the west and slowly fading to gunmetal blue. A breeze drifted in from the bayou, humid and smelling of water and fertile black earth mingled with the supper scents of spicy fish and sizzling meat.

He'd seen Franklin arrive in the back of a wagon surrounded by a dozen kids, while a fat little boy who'd looked about eight was tending the reins of a rather plump horse. The children had helped Franklin down – not an inconsiderable task -- then had taken some books from the wagon as if he'd been reading to them. There were also several hampers, indicating an ample lunch for Franklin and his young entourage, as well as a huge string of catfish. The fish were also rather fat, which somehow wasn't surprising.

"I'm glad you also noticed," said Skyler. "I was startin' to think I was dreamin' an' still on the horse with you."

"Well," said Cartwright, stripping naked and starting to wash. "The house boys at my ol' plantation was always puttin' on uppity airs whenever the massa weren't around. ...Lord, this water be turnin' black! That road was awful dusty, Sky. Don't 'magine nobody dream up dirt."

"Yeah," agreed Skyler, noting a ghostly impression of grime where Andrew had nestled against his chest. "Don't use all the soap." He turned from the window and added, "But, it seems a lot more than just silly airs. Lucky don't seem like he's playin' when he's doin' that gentleman stuff. ...In fact, it's the other way around; he seems like he's playin' at bein' a slave."

Cartwright soaped under his arms. "I notice that when I first met him, Sky. But I reckoned it 'cause he been raised in a house. Don't some massas educate slaves?"

"Some do," Skyler admitted. "An', yeah, I'm gonna educate you." He considered, then added. "An' here's another secret; Lucky can read!"

Cartwright didn't look shocked, or even pretend to be. "I kinda suspect that, Sky. But it somethin' most massas wouldn't suspect 'cause they wouldn't wanna believe it. Like animals can't be educated."

"The smart ones believe it," said Skyler, removing his boots and shucking his trousers. "More than believe it, they know it. An', between you an' me, it scares 'em."

"Even you?" asked Cartwright.

"It doesn't scare me personally, though sometimes I wonder it should." Skyler shrugged. "Maybe I got *too* educated. An' maybe I listened to things I shouldn't."

Cartwright scrubbed his chest with a cloth. "Mean you can be too educated?"

"One can be educated above their station in life."

Cartwright paused in his washing. "Mean, like if life was a railroad train, some people s'posed to get off at stations before they gets to the end of the line?"

"Somethin' like that," said Skyler. "It's called a metaphor, like the underground railroad."

"But, who be the conductors, Sky? On that metaphor railroad? Tellin' some people they got to get off an' can't go no further in life?"

"I used to think it was people with lots of education who knew what was best for other people, but now I ain't so sure. Maybe it's really the people who own an' run the railroad... metaphorically speakin'. ...But, educating slaves is like givin' 'em tools you can't take away."

"Like them cane-cuttin' blades?" asked Cartwright.

Skyler, now naked, turned back to the window. The sun had set, but a bloody red stripe like a gash from a whip still lingered on clouds in the darkening sky. "Exactly," he said. "You're givin' 'em potential weapons that could be used against you."

"They could also use 'em *for* you, Sky."

Skyler faced Cartwright again. "We're scared you won't forget all the bad... inhuman... things we've done to you. Like, what if Andrew had gotten away after what that... thing... did to him an' found me sleepin' in the woods? An' what if he had a cane-cuttin' blade?"

"But you ain't done inhuman things."

"But I know they happen," said Skyler. "An', by not doin' nothin' to stop 'em, I let 'em keep on happening."

"Sound like you scared of trustin' that we be human, too."

"It's like Lucky said tonight, about everything comes in all colors... good an' bad, kindness an' hate." Skyler took a match from a box and lit the Argand lamp. Then he laughed. "You got that wash-cloth black as sin."

"Dammit, I asked if you wanna go first."

"Turn around, I'll scrub your back."

"You does take real good care of me."

"Oh, shut up."

"Is sin always black?"

"It comes in all colors, too."

The boys completed their washing, Cartwright scrubbing Skyler's back and leaving the water the color of coal. They shared a towel to dry themselves, then Skyler glanced at their evening clothes he'd laid out on the bed. "You think Lucky was jokin' with us about not dressin' for supper? I'd feel like a fool comin' down there in buckskin an' findin' him dressed in a suit. That's just the kind of trick he'd pull."

Cartwright smiled. "'Least I be comfortable waitin' on you. 'Sides, like he say, it really too hot for spur-fool-us clothes. Damn if I see all the bother."

Skyler laughed. "I've thought the same for most of my life."

There was a timid tap on the door.

"Come in," called Skyler, and Andrew peeped in, a candle in hand. His iron collar had been removed, and he wore only trousers a little too large. It occurred to Skyler that he was the skinniest child at Content. He'd obviously had a bath, and his bushy hair had been lightly oiled and sparkled in the candle glow. It seemed very sad to Skyler that, even though clean and decently dressed, he still bore the brutal scars on his back, and would for the rest of his life.

"'Scuse me, massa," said Andrew. "I's s'posed to show y'all to supper. ...Um, how I do that?"

Skyler smiled. "You're doing it now. We just follow you."

"Well, then c'mon please, suh."

"Skyler," said Skyler.

"Oh, yeah, we's alone."

Chapter Twenty-One

Skyler had been prepared for more strangeness, but the scene in the dining room froze him in shock! He stopped in the doorway so suddenly that Cartwright bumped into him.

"'Scuse me, Sky."

"...Oh. Sorry, my fault," said Skyler, trying to recover his poise. He was certainly glad he hadn't dressed up because everyone else was nearly naked in only trousers or cotton shorts. He'd expected a kind of barbecue -- maybe with a "bayou theme" -- but this was just *impossible!* Here was a small but fine dining room in a modest but stately plantation house, a crystal chandelier ablaze, a huge table set with immaculate cloth, impressive silver and candle stands, and massively laden with marvelous food... yet everyone in it was black!

And not only black, but no older than he, while many were several years younger.

Well, he thought, it was Lucky's party. But still he had never imagined how such an event might actually look!

Still somewhat dazed, he studied the scene, noting the table was set for six. But, who were the masters and who were the slaves? Near-naked kids carried food from the kitchen, while others on tiptoes made finishing touches to silverware placement and settings. And Lucky sat at the head of the table in another of Franklin's enormous chairs.

"I's sure this ain't normal," said Cartwright.

"Maybe on some other planet," said Skyler.

He noticed the chair on Lucky's right had been bolstered with a cushion as if intended for somebody small. The next chair was already occupied by Danny's rolly bulk.

Lucky saw Skyler and got to his feet. "Pray have seats, gentlemen." He nodded to Andrew, who'd led Skyler in. "I hope the cushion will suit, young sir, in rising you to the occasion."

Then he gave Skyler a smile. "Here on my left, if you please, Sir Knight. I would have seated you on my right, but we have an unexpected guest... one might even call him a knight... who's been on a rather arduous quest and I know you'd want him to have that honor. ...And, Cartwright, the third chair, if you don't mind? Lucinda will be with us shortly and asks we start without her... still fussin' in the kitchen. You know how women are about food, everything must be perfect. I do hope you like catfish? Master Franklin caught 'em this morning. They're one of Lucinda's specialties."

"...Oh," said Skyler. "Yes, very much." Again he thought of the story by Poe, which seemed to be coming to life. Yet, everything here was really quite grand, including all the lavish food and many dishes of appetizers, while scents from the kitchen promised more, and possibly even greater delights.

"Sky," whispered Cartwright as they sat down, two smaller boys holding their chairs. "I gots too many choices in forks."

"Start from the outside and work your way in. The funny-lookin' one is for oysters."

"A nice little group," observed Lucky when everyone was seated, Andrew on the bolstered chair and gazing around in wonder at sights he'd probably never dreamed. Danny unfolded a napkin for him.

Skyler had heard a few stories of eccentric plantation masters, and Franklin seemed to be one. Of course, a master was God in his realm, and if he let slave children play in his house it wasn't for Skyler to judge.

Then he reconsidered. It would have been acceptable if Franklin had beaten or starved his slaves, or worked them to death in his fields, but for -- *this* -- he could be tarred and feathered!

And probably Skyler, too! This would be seen as mocking the masters! He wondered if he should get out of here before he got in deeper. Cartwright wouldn't tell anyone, not after Skyler explained to him what a *very* bad idea this was.

But, instead of escaping, he smiled across the snowy white linen. "Andrew, you're lookin' well tonight."

Andrew smiled, his big eyes bright. "I feels well, Sk... is this the same as if we was alone?"

"Yeah," said Skyler.

"I feels well, Skyler," said Andrew. He took a sip from a water glass of fine imported crystal. A boy, maybe seven, refilled it, standing on tiptoes to reach the table. "'Specially out that damn collar!"

"I imagine so," said Skyler, deciding he was in this now so he might as well enjoy it. A small boy filled his glass with beer, and it wasn't until he took a sip that he realized, if he had left, he wouldn't see Lucinda again.

"Have a smoked oyster," said Danny to Andrew, then studied Andrew's ravaged back as another boy offered the oyster tray. "Did they whip you a lot? Or was that for runnin'?"

"A lot," said Andrew, taking an oyster. "But the more scars you get the less it hurt."

"Try the *pâté*," said Lucky. "And the beer is really quite excellent. ...Did they ever flay the flesh off your bones?"

"A little," said Andrew, as a boy filled his glass. "But they sho' flay it off a friend of mine! Weren't much left we could bury."

"What was his offense?" asked Lucky.

"Stole a chicken from the massa."

"Ah," said Lucky. "A life for a life, to paraphrase the Bible."

"The chicken lived," said Andrew.

Cartwright sipped from his glass. "They used a whip with nails at my ol' place."

"That gotta hurt!" said Andrew. "Try them oysters, they real good. ...Ever get chained to a wagon wheel an' driven through a river?"

"No," said Cartwright. "But I got two days in the sweat box one time... too small to lay down in, too low to stand up. We had a little one just for kids."

"What was your offense?" asked Lucky.

"Walkin' 'cross the Big House lawn."

"Your master was kinder than some."

"No food or water I s'pose?" asked Danny.

"Nope. Lots flies an' skeeters, though. I 'bout got eaten alive in there. ...What this stuff, Sky?"

"Caviar. Spread it on one of those crackers."

"But what is it, Sky?"

"If you like it I'll tell you."

Cartwright lowered his voice. "What you gonna do to Remus for yankin' out that feather?"

"I'd like to give him a dollar."

Then Skyler turned to the kitchen door as Lucinda entered. His throat seemed to tighten a little, and he quickly got to his feet. The other boys also rose.

"Gentlemen," said Lucky. "Y'all know my sister Lucinda."

Andrew giggled. "Yeah, she gimmie a bath."

"Oh, except for Cartwright," said Lucky. "Lucinda, this is Cartwright. He's Skyler's squire, so I'd say he has great expectations."

Lucinda smiled her cute dimpled smile as Cartwright came over and took her hand. Her dress was a simple blue cotton shift, though it seemed like the finest of gowns to Skyler and showed off her figure beautifully as if it had been designed for her by the grandest salon in Paris. She exchanged greetings with Cartwright, and Skyler realized that his "squire" was really very handsome, but then Lucinda's eyes met his.

"Good evening, Sir Knight. You're lookin' well."

Skyler bowed and took her hand as Cartwright stepped aside. Part of his mind was appalled at this play -- his father would have been livid and his mother might have fainted -- but at the moment he didn't care. "And so are you, Milady. That dress is quite magnificent. And you wear it exquisitely well."

"Why thank you, sir." Lucinda seemed to restrain a giggle. "I so admire buckskin."

Lucky chuckled. "'Specially when there's a buck inside."

Lucinda smiled. "Do forgive my brother's wit."

"I often do," said Skyler.

Lucky laughed. "The other buck's got muscles that show... as Milady has no doubt observed... an' I'm sure he's just as smart. Wouldn't you like to give him a bath?"

"I just forgave him again," said Skyler.

"I hope you like catfish," said Lucinda.

"More than anything else in the world. Present company excepted."

Cartwright returned to his chair. A little boy waited to seat Lucinda, but Skyler performed that courtesy. The other boys resumed their places, and Lucky raised his beer glass. "Gentlemen and lady. A toast to Andrew, our guest of honor!"

Everyone drank. Andrew looked shy and probably blushed, though being so dark it didn't show.

"Speech please, Andrew," prompted Lucky.

"...Um..." said Andrew. "I's real glad to be alive an' with y'all tonight. This mornin' I's thinkin' I's gonna be dead 'fore the sun go down. An' I's grateful belongin' to Skyler now."

Now it was Skyler who blushed.

Supper was a swirl of impressions, dark happy faces, bright cheerful smiles, lots of laughter and fabulous food. The catfish were truly delicious, spicily breaded, fried in butter, and served on fluffy beds of rice, and Skyler meant every word of his praise. Like the last time he'd dined at Content, he ate until he felt ready to burst and the laces of his trousers were straining beneath his bulging belly. The candle flames seemed to glow golden and soft, lighting the scene with a dreamlike haze, and he felt sometimes as if was dining with an African prince in a Nubian court.

After peach pie with sweet whipped cream, Skyler could barely move. He seemed to gently awake from a dream when Lucinda spoke his name:

"How was everything, Skyler?"

Skyler sighed in pure content. "Positively meteoric!"

The room came gradually back into focus, revealing everyone else asleep, including Cartwright beside him. The "servants" were in the kitchen and seemed to be having their own little party with no doubt lavish leftovers. Lucky reclined with a smile on his face, fingers laced over his gigantic belly, and Danny slept in a similar pose like a slightly smaller mirror image.

"Did you cook it all, Lucinda?" asked Skyler.

"I had lots of help. An' my momma, of course."

"You could make a fortune in New Orleans opening a restaurant."

"Why, thank you Skyler. But, I'd have to be sold to someone down there."

"...Oh... yeah. I forgot. ...Very stupid of me."

"Very noble of you to rescue Andrew."

"I wouldn't have left a dog with that... thing. ...Sorry, I should have said that better."

"You did what you knew was right," said Lucinda. "That's how I think of noble."

"Thank you," said Skyler, then sighed. "But it's gonna be hard to keep bein' noble after I get him home."

"'We may do noble acts without ruling the earth and sea.'"

"You've read Aristotle?" asked Skyler.

"Only a bit."

"Um," said Skyler. "It seems very kind of Master Franklin to allow... events such as this."

"He's a very noble man," said Lucinda. Then she smiled and added, "And he's never let anyone hold that sword, except for Lucky, who keeps it polished."

"Then I feel doubly honored," said Skyler.

Lucinda looked at her slumbering brother. "You'll be having cigars and brandy as soon as he's finished his nap. I should be getting home."

"Don't you live in the house?" asked Skyler.

"We're quite comfortable in the Quarters... the village, as we call it." Lucinda turned to one of the windows, lit from without by a full silver moon. "And it's a beautiful night for a walk."

Walking was the last thing that Skyler wanted to do at the moment, yet he instantly got to his feet. His mind knew this was far from proper -- maybe as far as the earth from the moon -- but he bowed and offered his hand. "May I see you home, Milady?"

"I'd like nothing better, Sir Knight."

Chapter Twenty-Two

The night was still very warm but the silver-blue moonlight made it seem cooler. Fireflies winked in the shadows, frogs and insects boomed and chittered, and a horse in the stable whinnied softly as Skyler and Lucinda strolled along the whistling walk to a path around the cook house. Lucinda's bare feet and Skyler's soft boots were as quiet as cats as they passed through a shadowed grove of trees and emerged into moonlight again.

The Quarters did look like a village, as if people actually wanted to live there. The board-and-bat cabins were freshly painted and looked pristine in Luna's soft rays. They had glass in their windows, and curtains, with candle and lamplight glowing within. The flowers had surely been planted around them and weren't just growing wild.

Despite his happy haze of fullness and the sweet company of Lucinda, Skyler's mind considered facts and the economics of slavery. It was really a very precarious balance that teetered upon the shoulders of slaves but burdened the minds of their masters. It would take very little to topple that balance; and all he was seeing just *couldn't* exist! It was true that the Quarters at Diligence were long overdue for repairs, and his father could have managed them; but Diligence, even rich as it was, could never afford to make its Quarters as fine and -- village-like -- as these.

And, what would be the point? A horse didn't care if its stable was painted or curtains were hung in the windows. Of course the roofs shouldn't leak -- that made for unhealthy conditions, which made for unproductive slaves -- but, glass, curtains and paint for the Quarters? Completely out of the question!

Skyler pictured his father's slaves -- at least as many as he could remember -- they might have been given a *little* more food, but never so much that they could get fat. And, even if that was possible, they would have to be worked from dawn to dusk – more than they were already -- and even beyond by torch or moonlight, for Diligence to sustain them.

Slaves were not engines of unfeeling iron like the traction machines Cartwright had shown him; you couldn't just put them back in a shed until it was time for work again. They needed constant attention and care, had to be watched and accounted for twenty-four hours of every day from their cradles to their graves. And you had to consider their feelings: treat them too harshly, as Andrew had been, and they tried to run away. Treat them too kindly, as Franklin had done, and...

They started to act like human beings?

Skyler pondered what was seeing along with what he'd already seen. Franklin's system seemed to be working, however impossible that was. He lived in a modest but well-furnished house in which he permitted his slaves to "play," and dine on the most expensive foods, while he apparently fished all day with books and children for company. ...And where, and who, were his overseers? His house was kept by Lucinda with help from some of the children, whose older siblings and mothers and fathers maintained the plantation and worked in the fields. ..Unsupervised? That simply wasn't possible!

"A penny for your thoughts," said Lucinda.

"...Oh," said Skyler. "I'm sorry, I probably seem rather dull."

Lucinda smiled. "I don't find you dull."

"Milady is very forgiving. I'm so full of your wonderful food that everything seems like a dream tonight."

"I take that as a compliment, sir."

"Um... do you really like to cook?"

"Oh yes, it's one of my passions." Lucinda laughed and looked down at herself. "But I guess that shows."

Skyler laughed, too. "It certainly shows on your brothers."

"They're the best testaments to my art."

"Not to mention Master Franklin."

"Mother is quite artful, too. And of course she was cooking for many years before I came along."

"I think you're beautiful," said Skyler. "Beautiful an' fun."

"Fun?" asked Lucinda.

"...Um..." said Skyler. "I'm sorry. ...I'm not very good at talkin' to girls. ...Ladies I mean. ...I meant you'd be fun to be with. ...Um... you'd wanna do things... an' be fun to be doin' 'em with." Skyler wiped sudden sweat from his face. "I sound like an ass."

Lucinda laughed. "I'll take fun as a compliment, too. And I don't think you sound like an ass."

"...I guess you're contented here?"

Lucinda paused to gaze around... the moon above, the neat little "village," the pretty flowers everywhere. Skyler heard voices inside the cabins, the sleepy murmurs of children as mothers and fathers tucked them in... he assumed they all had real beds instead of straw pallets on rough wooden frames.

"It's a good place," said Lucinda. "And maybe I should be contented here. But I've never been out the front gates. I know there's a whole lot more to the world and I hope to see it some day."

Skyler didn't know how to reply: the world -- what little he'd seen so far -- was a long, *long* way from being content. Maybe as far as the earth from the moon. Even the people who should have been happy with all their wealth and property seemed discontented, wanted more, and were *still* unhappy if they got it. He almost asked why she wanted to travel when she already had a good life here -- a seemingly perfect life for a slave -- but that didn't seem right.

Then he almost asked if she'd like him to buy her, but that seemed a ridiculous question, not to mention distasteful... even if her brother had asked him. And that was even stranger! Lucky lived in luxury here; and Skyler still didn't know what he did except polishing an ancient sword, and "tellin' Massa Frankin his thinkin's."

"I think that myself sometimes," said Skyler.

"But, you've been out in the world."

"Just in New Orleans for a year. There's so many other places to see... France, of course, an' castles in England. Egypt, too."

"Egypt?" asked Lucinda.

128

"I always wanted to see the pyramids. An' the Sphinx."

Lucinda smiled again. "So have I. And I wouldn't mind a few castles, either."

"They even have castles in Africa... built by Africans, I mean... though most white people don't know it. Or maybe won't admit it."

"I know," said Lucinda. "I'd like to see a few of those, too."

"So would I," said Skyler.

They arrived at a fine little cabin. It was similar to the others, obviously built within this generation, though each seemed to have individual features. Each had a small, roofed porch in front, and all had chairs on the porches. There were swings in many trees, and toys on most of the porches; a rocking-horse, a rocking... lion? Little wagons and clever dolls.

The boards creaked softly beneath their feet as they climbed the single step, and a woman's voice called from inside: "Lucinda?"

"Yes, momma."

"Um," said Skyler. "Thank you for that excellent supper."

"My pleasure, sir," said Lucinda. "Although it was my brother's idea."

"He seems to have an abundance of them."

"Yes, he thinks quite a lot."

Skyler smiled. "And you, I more than suspect, do as well. ...It's part of why I think you're fun."

"That's a very nice word when you say it."

Skyler kept hold of Lucinda's hand. Her long-lashed eyes seemed to mirror the moon, and her full lips rested partly open, revealing a tempting crescent of white. Then, Skyler's arms went around her, with only her thin cotton dress between them. Their kiss lasted long, they tasted, explored; and only parted breathlessly when floorboards creaked inside the cabin as someone came to the door. There followed a pause as if to ponder, and finally the latch bar lifted. Lucinda's mother appeared, filling the doorway, eclipsing the lamplight, but smiling pleasantly... as any good mother would tactfully do when a certain amount of time had passed in a similar situation.

"Um," said Skyler. A suddenly very small part of his mind, in a petulant voice like a spoiled child's, squeaked that he had every right. But he slammed the nursery door in its face.

"Good evening," he said, stopping himself before saying "Missus." ...Missus, what? Very few slaves had second names; if they did, it was only a master's whim. One didn't give horses second names, and of course slaves had no family names. "Ma'am," he said, then added, "I was thanking Lucinda for the wonderful supper, though I understand you helped prepare it, and very delightfully so."

The big woman smiled again. "Only a bit, sir. Lucinda does quite well by herself."

"That is apparent," said Skyler. "Goodnight, Lucinda. And Ma'am."

"Goodnight, Sir Knight," said Lucinda, not seeming to think it sounded funny. "It's really been quite fun."

"Indeed it has, Milady."

Chapter Twenty-Three

"Sir, I would like to buy your boy Lucky, as well as his sister Lucinda. ...I hope you don't find my proposal offensive?"

Skyler had added the last part because of the silence that followed. It seemed to be a thoughtful pause, Franklin only smiling at him while puffing a fine cigar. They were seated in the library with cups of delicious coffee, after polishing off an enormous breakfast of sausage, eggs, and buttermilk pancakes, accompanied by slabs of toast with jam. The only sound was the patter of rain trickling down the windows; a cleansing kind of summer storm that would likely continue for most of the day and had filled the morning with scents of life.

Skyler could see the slaves outside cutting cane and tending the grounds at their usual leisurely pace. The children were simply playing again, most of them naked and splashing in puddles, or running and sliding across the lawn like glistening otters upon their bellies. He wondered if Andrew had ever played.

Skyler was clad in his buckskin trousers and linen shirt, his Indian boots on a hassock. He also held a cigar, and hovering ghosts of grays and blues drifted around the room. The watery light through the windows gave the sword a silver glow; and the silence continued except for the rain, as if Franklin was pondering deeper things instead of merely a business proposal. Finally, he asked, "Have you spoken with them?"

The question could have been absurd... or would have been anywhere else but Content. One didn't speak with an animal before asking its owner to sell it. But Skyler nodded and said:

"It was Lucky who asked me, sir. And I mentioned the subject, though indirectly, to Lucinda last night. She told me she's never been out your front gates."

Franklin looked thoughtful again. "Most of the children and younger people have never left Content, though I never discouraged them." He shifted his eyes to the rain-shimmered windows. "It's a very unjust world out there, and much more so for them. Many's the time I've considered the question of what gives us the right to enslave them."

"...Well, doesn't it say in the Bible, sir, that we may buy slaves from other lands?"

Franklin gave Skyler an ironic smile. "It also says in the Bible, sir, that anyone who works on the Sabbath must be put to death. Did you never work on a Sunday?"

"...I never considered that."

Franklin sighed smoke. "I have found many things in the Bible, sir, which remind me it was written by men, and often to further their own agendas... to subjugate others to their will and justify that to themselves... instead of actually serving God in the ways I imagine He'd want to be served."

"We desperately need a new cook," said Skyler. "I admit that's part of my agenda."

Franklin chuckled. "Begging your pardon, Master Knight, but that's hardly the way to negotiate. If your horse had died somewhere on a road while pulling a wagon of perishables, you would not mention that to a seller when asking to purchase another steed."

"Well, 'course not, sir," said Skyler. "But I have no wish to deceive you."

Franklin took a sip of coffee. "I can well understand why you'd fancy Lucinda. She has many impressive qualities besides her cooking skills. ...She also paints, you know?"

"No, sir, I didn't," said Skyler, surprised.

"Astounding talent, I think."

Skyler gazed around the room at the many fine landscapes and portraits of children. "Did she paint these?"

"Indeed she did," said Franklin. "I've sold her works in New

Orleans, and the buyers have been quite ecstatic, though unaware she's 'only a slave.' ...But, why in heaven would you want to buy Lucky?"

"Master Franklin!" cried Lucky, appearing in the doorway, as usual barely in trousers. "You know I'm very useful!"

Franklin laughed. "You're also a very good listener."

"I was comin' to see if you wanted more coffee."

"Of course you were," said Franklin.

Lucky lumbered up to Skyler. "I could assist with your correspondence."

Skyler smiled. "I don't have much of that."

"You will," said Lucky. "Not only business, but after you start traveling you're gonna have friends all over the world."

"I can't see much hope of traveling, no matter how much I want to. And, having a slave who can read and write... at least in this part of the world... could get both of us in a lot of trouble."

Franklin snubbed out his cigar. "It's not, as I expect you know, unheard of to have a literate slave; it's just not freely admitted. But you already have an excellent squire... one who can actually get on a horse... and seems a pleasant companion as well."

Skyler smiled again. "And never far away. ...C'mon in, Cartwright. And you might as well bring Andrew."

"Who could be a burden for you," said Franklin, as Cartwright and Andrew entered.

Skyler put out his cigar. "I've been thinking a lot about Andrew, sir. But I couldn't have left him... in that situation."

"No decent human being would have." Franklin smiled at Andrew. "Come here, son."

Andrew came timidly over, and Franklin studied his back. "And we call ourselves a 'superior race!'" He patted Andrew's shoulder. "Sit down over there, if you please."

"On a chair, suh?"

"Of course. There is a plate of Lucinda's cookies, and a book if you like."

"A... book, suh? But I can't read."

"It's a picture book about lions."

"Thank you, suh."

"And ring for a glass of milk if you wish."

"*Me* ring, suh?"

"Allow me," said Lucky, waddling over to the rope.

Franklin faced Skyler again. "But, you can't show him kindness or your other slaves will get ideas."

Skyler sighed. "I'm all too aware of that, sir. It's a burden I brought on myself."

Franklin nodded as a small girl entered and Lucky asked for a glass of milk. "We often create our own burdens in life, and sometimes by doing what's right."

Cartwright came up to Skyler. "I can understand, Sky, if you rather have Lucky instead of me."

Franklin laughed. "I surely can't!"

Cartwright went on, "But, please don't sell me away, Sky! I can work in your blacksmith shop. Or anythin' else you want me to do."

"Oh, quit talkin' nonsense," said Skyler. "You're more than my boy, you're my..." He suddenly felt ashamed at almost having said 'companion.' "Friend," he finished, and felt proud to say it.

"You're my friend, too," said Cartwright.

Franklin smiled. "A true friend is something of priceless value, as well as a rarity in life, and can never be bought or owned."

"I'm sure of that, sir." Skyler reached for Cartwright's hand, and Cartwright took his tightly.

"You can't have too many, either," said Lucky. "And there's plenty of me for both of you."

"So we's noticed," said Cartwright.

Skyler got up to throw an arm over Lucky's shoulder, and Cartwright did the same. Lucky grasped them both around their waists. "All for one, and one for all!"

"Perhaps we may make an arrangement," said Franklin. "But first, Master Loki, if you don't mind, would you ask Lucinda to join us?"

Chapter Twenty-Four

"Careful dammit, Sky!" warned Danny. "You gonna get branded worse than Andrew!"

To Skyler it seemed a miracle that Danny hadn't been "branded," considering all his rolly bulk spilling everywhere: yet he seemed at home in the blacksmith shop with its roaring forge and leaping flames as he and Skyler, Cartwright and Andrew, strug-gled to lift the wagon tire, a circle of red-hot glowing iron about six feet in diameter and weighing nearly a hundred pounds. Each boy was equipped with a pair of tongs, but only the sweat of their shirtless bodies shielded their skins from the heat.

"Careful now!" warned Danny again. "Don't tip it, Andrew! ...Skyler, a little higher! It gotta be set on straight!"

Skyler wished Danny could move a bit faster, because his tongs were growing warm as they carried the tire horizontally to a wagon wheel on wooden blocks. Skyler was more than a little relieved when they finally mounted the tire and doused it with buckets of water. Steam burst up in a hissing cloud, filling the smoke-blackened, three-sided shed like swirling mist in a swamp. Skyler and Andrew backed away in fear of being scalded, but Danny and Cartwright studied the wheel and Cartwright smiled at Danny.

"That gonna be a perfect fit."

"Never throwed a tire yet." Danny leaned close to the steaming wheel, its heavy spokes creaking and popping as the iron band contracted. "Never busted a wheel neither. You forge a tire a little too small an' the spokes gonna split the rim when it shrink."

"Don't I know it," Cartwright agreed. "The blacksmith boy at my

Jess Mowry

ol' place got a whippin' for that."

"This call for a beer," puffed Danny. "An' after lunch we mount the wheel." He smiled at Skyler, who'd stepped outside to cool himself in the pattering rain. "Then I take y'all home. ...You gonna feed me supper, of course?"

"All you can eat," said Skyler. "Though it won't be near as fine as the banquet we had here last night."

"I notice that," said Danny. "'Course, you got my sister now."

Skyler gazed through the rain to the "village," where Lucinda and Lucky were packing their things in their parents' cabin. That seemed funny... the concept of slaves having things to pack, or at least enough to require several trunks, which was why they were taking a big freight wagon instead of Franklin's buggy. The wagon had needed a wheel repaired, so Danny had forged a new tire. "We can't ask her to cook tonight. It'll be dark by the time we get home, an' she'll need to get settled in."

Danny tugged at his slipping trousers. "You a good man for thinkin' that way."

"He good as Massa Franklin," said Andrew, who stood cooling off beside Skyler.

Skyler ruffled the boy's wet hair. "What would you know about that? You belonged to me for less than a day."

"I knows a good man when I sees one," said Andrew, "'cause I seen lots of bad ones."

Cartwright smiled. "I knowed it, too, first time I met him."

Skyler laughed. "Now y'all soundin' like Lucky with all his talk about knowin' things I don't even know myself."

Danny said, "With my sister cookin', you might end up lookin' like Lucky." His smile seemed to turn a bit sly. "You got a bargain on both of 'em, Sky."

Skyler couldn't argue with that, recalling the morning's events. They had all sat down in the library to work out the "arrangement." Lucinda and Lucky weren't for sale, but Franklin had suggested a trade... Andrew!

There had, however, been conditions: foremost of these was Skyler's word that the twins could always return to Content any time the wished. Likewise, they could visit their parents, and invite Danny to visit them. Despite their sitting beside him, Skyler had pondered that. In a way it seemed perfectly reasonable, and yet it defied everything he'd been taught... though a lot of things were defying those teachings since he'd first met Lucky. Of course, his mother would be delighted with Lucinda's marvelous meals, and Lucky could help with those dammable "books," which would please his father. And, Andrew would have a much better life here than Skyler could have given him.

Chapter Twenty-Five

"**L**ucinda?" asked Skyler. "Why didn't you tell me you painted pictures? 'Specially such pretty ones."

He was tending the reins of a pair of plump horses who waddled along puffing and blowing, pulling the lumbering wagon, his own horse ambling behind on a ten-foot tether, though he could have pulled the wagon alone and never broken a sweat. Soft rain still fell in the steamy night, and mist obscured the moss-bearded trees which overhung the road. The bulls-eye lamp on the front of the wagon threw a yellow glow ahead, making the raindrops glisten like gold. The only sounds were the splashing of hooves through flooded ruts, and the rumble and creak of massive wheels. The wagon's cover had been set up -- mainly to protect the trunks because nobody minded the gentle rain -- and the other boys all lay asleep beneath its canvas shelter. It was really Danny's duty to drive, but the boy couldn't manage to stay awake, so Skyler had taken command.

It felt good to be shirtless out in the rain, warm as it trickled off his hat and ran in rivulets down his back. Lucinda was seated beside him, draped in Skyler's oilskin cloak and had been remarking at all the new sights as they splashed and jolted along. Lunch had of course been delicious, then they had mounted the wagon wheel and loaded Lucinda's and Lucky's trunks. Night was settling in by the time they had reached Knight's Crossing, and Lucinda had gazed at the tiny town as if it was Paris or London.

"Why is it called Knight's Crossing?" she'd asked, as they'd rolled past lamp and candle-lit windows down its single muddy street. "What is there to cross?"

Skyler had explained that almost a hundred years ago his family had built a bridge across the local river. ...Actually, their slaves had built it. But he didn't say that, though it probably didn't need saying.

He'd thought about stopping in town, but realized there was nowhere to go except to the back of the tavern. For once in his life he felt *very* white, and in a very shameful way. He had four friends aboard this wagon, but only *he* could have gone inside any of those shops and stores. If the rain had been cold instead of warm, if they had been tired and hungry, only *he* could have sat by a fire, ordered a meal or rented a room.

It had come as a shock to realize, that even with all his family's wealth, he couldn't have decently cared for his friends. He might have ordered the tavern-keeper to set up a table in a back room, but people would have talked, and his own name would have been blackened. Poor whites would call him a nigger-lover -- even if not to his face -- and proper people would snub him.

But, it would cut much deeper than that; his parents would also be punished. Polite excuses would be made for not attending his mother's parties. The stores would often be "out" of things. Mail would start getting "lost" coming or going from Diligence. Telegrams wouldn't arrive, and shipments on the railroad would be misrouted or delayed. In a way he, too, was a slave -- even if a privileged one -- trapped in a system of wrong upon wrong. Like shoring up a rotten old bridge -- you were only keeping it standing awhile before it finally collapsed -- and he'd only paused at the edge of town to light the lamp and check his horse.

Lucinda smiled at him now, her chubby face shining like polished jet in the flickering glow of the lamp. "You never asked, Sir Knight."

"As Milady knows, I haven't been knighted. ...And I wouldn't be worthy."

"Why not? You're certainly brave and noble."

Skyler sighed. "No I'm not." He glanced through the trees where a candlelit window revealed the last of the dwellings that lay around the town. "I'm just as scared as everyone else of what this place could do to me. I'm not brave enough to fight those dragons, nor strong enough to slay 'em."

Lucinda smiled again. "I'd say you've inflicted a few wounds."

"If so, they're very small," said Skyler, "and haven't yet roused the beast on me. ...But, about your painting, I just never thought..."

"That a slave would have any hobbies?"

"I wouldn't have put it that way. Besides, they're too good to call a hobby." Skyler laughed. "My mother has hobbies, as you'll find. And pray you're not subjected to any."

"I also play the piano."

"...That's wonderful!"

"So does Lucky."

"Well damn! ...Um, 'scuse me." Skyler looked over his shoulder where Lucky's black mass was a shadow in shadows, asleep with Cartwright and Danny. "Mother's been tryin' to learn it for years. Dad leaves the house whenever she plays. ...So do the cats, come to think of it."

"Then there's another use for my brother, helping your mother refine her hobby. ...That's not against the law, is it? Slaves being able to play the piano?"

"Never heard tell," said Skyler, flicking the reins a little to speed up the leisurely horses. "But it's nobody's business."

"Because a master is God in his realm?"

Skyler shook his head. "God created man in His image, but who are we to define that image and give to it a color? Or to claim we're doing His will for anything other than earthly gain."

Chapter Twenty-Six

"**Y**ou live in a castle, Sir Knight!"

Skyler smiled as the heavy wagon lumbered up the graveled drive between the rows of neatly-trimmed hedges. The manicured lawns stretched away on each side, glistening under the gentle moon as the clouds began to break overhead. The huge pond shimmered like mercury, and the trees and shrubs wore sparkling jewels. He glanced at the towering three-story house with its massive columns and vast portico glimmering as white as bone. He'd never paid it much attention; simply a house in which he'd grown up, sliding down banisters, running through halls, playing with Romulus and Remus -- who used to be the fan boys then -- but now he imagined it looked much different, seen though Lucinda's ebony eyes.

"It's as big as a castle," he said. "'Least the ones I've seen in pictures. Got a whole bunch of rooms we don't even use, and I used to call the cellar a dungeon." He regarded the mansion again. "My grandfather wanted a lot of kids, but I'm the only inheritor now." Then he smiled. "S'pose I should raise up a big bunch to fill it." He stopped himself before adding that a hundred slaves had labored to build it. He'd said that with pride for most of his life, but now it seemed nothing to boast about.

"Any prospects?" asked Lucinda.

"Huh?"

"For filling your castle with kids, Sir Knight."

Skyler shrugged. "I met a few girls in New Orleans... mother gave me introductions an' wired my aunt to follow 'em up. Tell you the truth, they bored me to tears. Always talkin' 'bout parties an' clothes, an' the latest fashions in Paris an' such. ...Bunch of silly malarkey, an' none of 'em know how to have any fun."

"What do you call fun, Sir Knight?"

"...Well... ridin' an' fishin' an' swimmin' are fun." Skyler laughed. "Even just climbin' trees, though reckon I'm gettin' too old for that."

Lucinda laughed, too. "It's been a while since I climbed a tree, but I go fishin' with Lucky and Danny. Swimmin', too, on occasion. I guess that isn't forbidden here?"

"'Course not," said Skyler. "I hope I can come along. ...In proper attire, of course."

"I do admire buckskin."

"Ever been on a horse?" asked Skyler.

"A few times. I imagine you get quite a view up on yours."

"I'll take you for rides anytime you want. Maybe you'd get more painting ideas."

"I like painting children at play."

"...Well... they don't play as much here." Skyler looked at the house again. "You'll be living inside, of course. The cook has a room off the kitchen. ...It's really quite nice."

"I'm sure it is," said Lucinda. "But, what about Betty? I wouldn't feel right displacing her."

"That won't be a problem," said Skyler. "She was never moved up from the Quarters."

"I'll want her to work with me. I'm sure I can teach her new skills."

"...Oh," said Skyler. "Of course."

The crunching of gravel beneath the wheels had awakened the boys in back. Cartwright looked out from under the cover. "We there yet, Sky?"

"Just about," said Skyler.

"Now, that's what I call a house!" said Lucky.

Danny yawned. "Biggest ol' house in the parish. Take twenty slaves just to dust it."

A peacock screeched in a nearby tree. "What the devil was that?" asked Lucky.

Skyler laughed. "Somethin' I wish was at the devil."

A lamp on a chain lit the huge front porch, and warm light shone from several windows. Skyler flipped open his watch: it was only a little past nine. He fingered the reins as they neared the house, not sure how to make his arrival. A freight wagon wasn't proper in front and should have been driven around to the stables. Slaves weren't allowed to use the front doors -- the butler, of course, but nobody else -- though Jupiter often "forgot," but Skyler decided he'd be dammed if he'd make his friends come in through the back!

Reaching a fork in the wide, curving drive, he tugged the reins to the right, and the battered old wagon rolled up to the steps as if it was the fanciest coach.

A boy was always on duty to watch, though they usually fell asleep at night; but Skyler heard scampering footsteps inside above the puffing breaths of the horses. He considered donning his shirt, but descended to earth without doing so. He assisted Lucinda down, then he and Cartwright helped Lucky and Danny. Billy arrived a few moments later, out of breath in just his trousers. He gaped at Lucky, clearly astonished, but then recovered his poise.

"Evenin', Massa Knight. Y'all have a good time at Content?"

"A very fun time, thank you, Billy. ...This is Lucinda, she'll be our new cook. Y'all know Danny, an' this is Lucky."

Billy regarded the mammoth boy. "What he be, suh?"

"...Lucinda's brother."

"Pleased to meet y'all," said Billy, then clambered up on the wagon seat.

Skyler added, "Get someone to unload those trunks and bring 'em into the house."

"Sho', Massa Knight." Billy looked down at the other kids. "Y'all can ride on back with me."

"That's all right, Billy," said Skyler, and took Lucinda's hand.

Billy looked astonished again, but unlatched the brake, flicked the reins, and the wagon rumbled away.

Still holding Lucinda's hand, Skyler led her up on the porch, the other boys following. The doors swung open majestically, spilling forth a fan of light. The butler looked more than a little perplexed, eyeing the four half-naked boys, especially the enormous Lucky, and Lucinda clad in Skyler's cloak.

"...Uh ...Evenin', Masta Knight." The man hesitated. "Uh... maybe the... others... would be more... comfortable... if I had someone take 'em 'round back?"

"Evenin', Jacob," said Skyler. "Everyone here is quite comfortable just as they are, thank you."

"...Uh, yes, Masta Knight."

"S'pose we're too late for supper?" asked Lucky.

Jacob didn't seem able to categorize Lucky; was he only a slave, a privileged slave... or one of those fabled free black people he'd no doubt heard stories about? And if the latter, how did you treat them? "...Uh... supper already been served, I fear."

"I'd fear it, too," said Skyler. "Another banquet of candied swill?"

"Y'all know how it been, suh."

"Don't I just," said Skyler. "But I think we're all in for a pleasant surprise. May I present Lucinda, who has consented to do us the honor of creating culinary delights."

Jacob hesitated, but then gave Lucinda a brief formal bow. "Pleased... er, Miss."

"Lucinda, will do," said Lucinda.

"And this is Lucky," said Skyler. "Who has consented to do me the honor of sharing his many thoughts... an' whether I want 'em or not."

"...Lucky," said Jacob, now clearly at sea as to what Lucky was.

"And of course you know Danny."

"Of course," said Jacob coldly. Then he hesitated again. "Uh... Masta Knight. I think I should mention, your father been a bit upset ever since just after supper."

"Was it that bad?"

"...Uh... possibly, suh. He been in the library ever since."

"'Least he ain't been on the pot."

Then Jupiter came out of the house, dressed as always in shabby old trousers and faded blue shirt. Greetings and introductions were made.

"Thank you, Jacob," said Skyler. "Will you see about the trunks as soon as Billy has them unloaded? Lucinda will be in the cook's room, of course."

"Yes, Masta Knight."

"Put Lucky's things in the room next to mine."

"Hey," said Lucky. "Thought I be stayin' with you and Cartwright."

"There's connecting doors." Skyler turned back to Jacob. "And see about Danny's accommodations. Please be sure he's comfortable."

"He can stay with me," said Lucinda.

"I's hungry," said Danny.

"We all are," said Skyler.

"Yes, suh," said Jacob. "I'll have somethin' laid out."

Skyler glanced at Jupiter, who seemed to be signaling him. "Y'all go with Jacob," he said to the others. "I'll join you in..." He looked at Jacob. "...the dining room."

Jacob raised an eyebrow. "Should I wake up the fan boys, suh?"

"No."

"Uh... who will serve, Masta Knight?"

Lucinda stepped forward. "Show me the kitchen, please. I think I can manage a supper for five." She indicated her brothers. "I do that feeding these two every day."

Cartwright said, "An' I, suh, shall serve it."

"An' I, suh, shall assist," said Lucky.

"An' I, suh, shall eat it," said Danny.

"...This way," said Jacob, looking confounded.

Lucky gave Skyler a nudge. "Another small wound, Sir Knight."

"In this case a very small dragon."

"Lord, Sky!" said Jupiter, when everyone else had left. "Your daddy been like to pitch a conniption!"

"Was supper that awful?"

"I's had better for a fact. But I think it somethin' he read in the paper. New one 'rive from 'Nawlins today an' he look about fit to conip when he read it."

"Maybe the price of cane went down? Or the ship came in with that new piano... the great big one he's been dreading?" said Skyler.

"I 'spect it be powerful loud. I'll go see him now. I got some news that'll cheer him up, Lucinda's gonna be cookin' for us."

Jupiter still looked doubtful. "Maybe you should dress up a bit in light of your daddy's mood."

"It's all right, Juppy."

The library was filled with cigar smoke, hazing the glow of a single lamp. A fire burned in the huge brick hearth despite the steamy warmth of the night, and his father sat in a big leather chair seeming to ponder the flames. Several cigar ends lay in a tray, and the brandy decanter was almost empty.

"Good evening, sir," said Skyler, removing his dripping hat as he entered.

"...Oh." The man turned to face him. If he noticed Skyler was shirtless and wet, he didn't give any sign. "Good evening, son, I'm glad you're here. Come have a drink, I have something to tell you. You'll find the cigars in their usual place."

"I was just about to have supper, sir."

"I won't keep you long. ...How was your stay at Content?"

"Very productive, sir. And I have some wonderful news."

"I'd surely be glad to hear some."

"Is something the matter, father?"

The man indicated a newspaper and sighed as Skyler read the front page. "If those God-dammed Abolitionists don't stop making trouble down here, I believe there is going to be a war."

"Huh?" said Skyler. "A war with who?"

"The North, son. The northern states. ...I wish they were all at the devil! And Abraham Lincoln foremost!"

Skyler put down the paper. "How can that be? I know they don't want slavery, but we're all part of the same country. How can a country fight itself?"

His father crushed out his cigar. "There's been talk of the southern states seceding from the Union. It's becoming a popular notion down here."

"Making two Americas?"

"Yes, son. Ours, as proposed, would be The Confederate States of America. The only question is, could we do it peacefully, or would we have to fight for our freedom?"

The man considered, then added, "If there was a war, it wouldn't be a long one. Just a few weeks at most, I'm sure. Once the North saw we were resolute they would back down very quickly. Wars, after all, are expensive. They waste a country's resources and kill many fine young men. But, the South will have to increase its production to prepare itself for war... cotton and wool for uniforms, leather for our soldiers' boots, horses, mules, and food of course. We'll have to work the slaves much harder, which will include our own."

He took another sip from his glass. "And they won't be willing to work if they hear the North wants to set them free. ...God help us all if that ever happened! And there are sure to be agitators stirring up trouble amongst our slaves. We'll have to start watching them very closely. You'll have to spend more time in the fields."

"What about doing the books?"

"I suppose I shall have to hire someone."

"Oh," said Skyler thoughtfully.

His father went on: "Any sign of reluctance to work or questioning our authority, any disobedience or even rumors of rebellion, cannot be allowed and must be punished! There must never be the slightest doubt that we are in control..." He stopped as one of the maids peeped in.

"Will you be wantin' soda, suh?"

"Not tonight, thank you, Bess." The man listened as the pad of slippers faded away up the hall, then said, "I may have a new whipping post set up, though hopefully just as a warning."

Skyler asked, "Does mother know about all this?"

"Of course not, son. She is only a woman and couldn't understand these things. She's been very happy planning your party. ...And I must insist you'll have it. You've been home for over a week and people are wondering about you."

"I often wonder myself," said Skyler.

His father rose and gripped Skyler's shoulders. "You shouldn't, son, you're a fine young man." He smiled. "A noble Knight, forgive the pun. And beneath that cherubic exterior I know you're very strong and brave."

"Thank you, sir," said Skyler. "I hope I may prove to be."

His father smiled again. "But, what is your good news, son?"

Chapter Twenty-Seven

"That was positively meteroic!" said Skyler, putting a last dish away. Though his father's words had been ominous, they were far from Skyler's mind right now here in the kitchen after supper. Despite what they'd said about serving themselves -- Lucky setting the table, and Skyler and Cart-wright bringing in food while Danny sat eagerly waiting -- Jacob had taken the liberty of providing Lucinda with scullery help, a sleepy girl of maybe eleven. She had begun to wash the dishes -- something she might have done in her sleep -- but Lucinda had sent her back to bed, and she and Skyler had finished the job.

"Thank you," said Lucinda, who was looking through drawers and cupboards inspecting her new domain. "But it was just dressing up leftovers."

"Mother will be delighted by anything you make." Skyler made a face. "'Specially with that party she's planning."

Lucinda closed a cupboard. "Your homecoming party? You don't seem very enthusiastic. Parties are supposed to be fun."

"Lucky's party was fun," said Skyler. "'Specially 'cause you were there. I wish you could be at this one... with me. We'd have fun pokin' fun at the peacocks, and I don't mean the kind with feathers."

Lucinda laughed. "That sounds like fun. But I'm sure there must be nice people, too."

"They might look nice, like a peacock looks nice, but then they sneak up an' peck your behind." Skyler turned to a window where the moon shone bright in a starry sky. "There's gotta be places in the world where things like that could happen... you an' me goin' to parties together. An' with *real* friends of ours no matter what color they are."

"We already did at Content."

"I meant someplace where it's normal. Where it's right an' how it should be."

"I understand," said Lucinda.

It was getting close to eleven o'clock. Danny, thoroughly stuffed with food, was asleep on a cot in Lucinda's room. Cartwright and Lucky had gone upstairs. Skyler's parents had also retired, and the house was dark and quiet. Somewhere out in the steamy night two trusted slaves patrolled the Quarters armed with ancient Brown Bess muskets... Skyler's father had doubled the watch in fear of agitators.

Skyler hung up a dish cloth. "You don't have to do miracles every day. My parents will be quite satisfied with food that doesn't oink, cackle, moo, baa, jump off its plate or require a funeral."

Lucinda inspected a knife for sharpness. "I'll serve up a passable breakfast tomorrow, followed by a decent lunch, and save the miracles for supper."

"Um?" asked Skyler. "Is your room all right?"

"Yes, thank you. And I enjoyed the trip through town."

"It sure wasn't London or Paris."

"It's the first town I've ever seen. Like starting small and working up."

"I wish it was a better place."

"Looked very nice to me."

"That's not what I meant," said Skyler. "In London or Paris we could have stopped and had a beer or somethin' to eat."

Lucinda touched Skyler's shoulder with the broad side of the knife. "Even a brave and noble knight can't right every wrong by himself."

"There's so many wrongs around here I wouldn't know where to start."

"Start small and work your way up, just as you've been doing." Lucinda put the knife in a rack. "Where's the bridge your family built?"

"It's farther up the road from here. We can ride there when you have time, if you like."

"That would be fun," said Lucinda. "'Course, I'm gonna be busy the next few days getting used to all this."

"I keep forgetting," said Skyler.

"Didn't I say I love to cook? It's an art everyone can appreciate."

"You really do?"

"I really do."

"Well, except for..." Skyler made another face. "...parties... you're only cooking for mother and dad. An' me of course, an' Cartwright... an' Lucky. ...With enough leftover for Jacob. An' Jupiter when he has a mind. ... Plus enough to 'disappear.'" Skyler frowned. "That's a lot."

"I'll have Betty to help." Lucinda laughed again. "And probably more other help if you have twenty people just to keep up this house. At Content there were only momma and me."

"But, didn't you just cook for Franklin? An' obviously Lucky an' Danny?"

Lucinda smiled a "Lucky" smile. "Master Franklin often has guests."

"But, I heard he didn't entertain. ...You don't mean his slaves?"

"Mostly the kids. He likes a jolly table."

"Can't say I'm all that surprised, said Skyler. "Not with him lettin' those kids look at books and takin' 'em fishin' every day. But it's good for his sake he's way out in the swamp and nobody knows much about him."

"So I've heard," said Lucinda, then began to put out the lamps. "How early is breakfast?"

"Compared to Content it's more like lunch. Father rises early, but has coffee with the overseers while listening to their reports. Then he rides out to check on the work. But mother won't be down until ten when father returns an' breakfast is served."

"I can surely live with that."

Skyler looked out the window again. "The moon's even bigger tonight."

"I'll miss that walk," said Lucinda. "From the house to the village. I did a lot of thinking out there. And more than a little dreaming."

"You mean about seein' the world?"

"That, and a lot of other things I'd guess most girls dream about."

"...Um, boys?" asked Skyler.

Lucinda smiled again. "Most girls dream about young men... at least if they have any sense."

"...Well, I 'spect you're tired."

"Are you suggesting a walk, Sir Knight?"

"...Well... it's kinda wet, Milady."

"But still very warm."

"Um... there's a sittin' house out by the pond. The moon always looks real nice on the water."

"I believe I'd like to see it, sir."

Skyler lit a candle and took Lucinda's hand. Together they walked through the vast silent house, past many doorways and shadow-filled rooms. The boy at the front doors lay asleep. Trading smiles, they tiptoed past him and out beneath the portico lamp. The moon shone bright on the expanse of lawn, which sparkled with millions of raindrop jewels. The air was pleasantly warm, filled with scents of flowers and grass, and the sweetness of cane in the fields. Feathers of mist floated over the pond, where bullfrogs boomed from lily pads and painted turtles paddled in the dancing glow of fireflies.

The sitting house was simply a shelter, a shingled roof without any walls, covered with garlands of glistening vines and built to offer shade from the sun. Skyler's mother used it a lot, watching the peacocks on hot afternoons, reading a book or a magazine while being fanned by one of the boys and sipping lemonade. There were wicker chairs inside, a table for drinks, and a big wooden chest.

"This is pretty," said Lucinda. "Like pictures of tropical islands. A person could live in a place like this."

"Reckon I could," said Skyler. "I fished in that pond a few times. When I was younger, of course. Got the fattest ol' carp you ever saw, gold ones imported from China. ...See there?"

"Oh, yes! They're beautiful! But I didn't know people ate them."

Skyler laughed. "I only did once. Me an' Remus. We were both about seven. Father caught us cookin' one an' I couldn't sit down for a week."

"What happened to Remus?"

"I was the only one who got whopped. 'Cause I was supposed to know better." Skyler regarded the moonlit water. "My father isn't a bad man, Lucinda, not cruel or malicious or hateful. He's just a part of a system that is. But I guess he's been taught... or taught himself... not to think about it."

Going into the shelter, Skyler opened the chest. "Here's something we can sit on." He spread a fluffy quilt on the floor, and they sat down together to gaze at the pond with its peaceful life and mirrored moonlight.

Skyler said, "Ain't nothin' much in it belongs around here... not the fish nor those big lily pads. Even the turtles from somewhere else. Keeps Romulus an' Remus busy snaggin' out natural things. ...I didn't mean to spoil it for you."

Lucinda smiled. "You didn't. It's still nice to look at."

"Yeah," agreed Skyler. "Just like your paintings... and just like you."

Skyler's hand found Lucinda's. He was very aware of her body beside him. "Um?" he asked. "Can I kiss you again, Milady? Like we did last night?"

"I believe I'd like that, sir. Very much."

They moved close together, and Skyler's arms went around her. Like the previous night, their kiss lasted long. But now they were alone and free, and no one would come to the door. They finally parted, both breathing hard, then kissed again even longer.

Chapter Twenty-Eight

Skyler ran up the stairs to his room feeling as light as a feather. Part of him wanted to shout and laugh, and yet he felt peaceful inside. The connecting doors were open, and lamplight shone in Lucky's room, but Lucky was lounging with Cartwright, both just in trousers on Skyler's bed and smoking expensive cigars. Cartwright had a bottle of brandy, and Lucky was reading the New Orleans paper.

"It's impossible, Sky," said Lucky, looking up as Skyler came in. "As I was just tellin' Cartwright."

"What is?" asked Skyler, shucking his boots as the other boys made room for him to nestle in between them.

"For the South to win if there's a war," said Lucky, laying the paper aside. "In fact, it's just plain foolish for you to even consider a war."

Skyler frowned, settling into the pillows, his shoulders pressed to Cartwright's and Lucky's. "I'm not considering a war." He lowered his voice a little and glanced to the hallway door. "An' you shouldn't be sayin' things like that. Not where slaves might hear. ...Why couldn't we win a war?"

"Care for a drink?" asked Cartwright, offering the bottle.

"Thanks." Skyler regarded the label, then took a swig and frowned at Lucky. "What makes you think you're so smart? ...Or white folks are stupid?"

"Present company excepted," said Lucky. "Though you do need a little more education."

"No doubt you been givin' Cartwright a lot."

"Want me to leave?" asked Cartwright.

"It's probably too late. This bed fairly reeks of breedin' ideas, an' you're no doubt impregnated."

"I try an' not let it show."

"You'll find that becomes more difficult as you get farther along."

"Want a cigar?" asked Lucky.

"Why not, they're father's, just like the brandy."

Lucky lit a cigar from the lamp, puffed it to life and passed it to Skyler. "What does this plantation produce? ...Besides a lot of bad ideas."

"For sellin'?" said Skyler. "Mostly cane."

"An' the other plantations around here?"

"More cane, rice, and beans. The ones farther north grow cotton and flax."

Lucky blew out a gray ghost of smoke. "None of that stuff can win a war, Sky. You've got an agrarian economy. That means..."

"I know what it means, and we've prospered from it."

"But, you made it dependent on captive and unwilling workers." Lucky smiled. "As Franklin already told you. ...But, it's guns win wars. It's cannons win wars. And ships with guns. And superior ships are powered by steam, which means they need engines of iron and steel made in modern factories, just like guns and cannons. And the South doesn't have many factories. ...May I...?"

"...Oh, sorry." Skyler passed the bottle to Lucky. "But, we can sell crops to buy what we need."

"Sell 'em to who?" asked Lucky, returning the bottle to Skyler, who drank and passed it to Cartwright. "Not to the North if there's a war. And it's mostly the North been buyin' your crops. And, if they blockade your harbors, you can't sell your things to other countries, or import what you need for a war."

For a moment Skyler felt anger; anger at Lucky for disrespecting a way of life in which he'd grown up; a way of life he'd been taught was noble... but also anger at himself for all he'd done to betray it lately.

He turned to the moonlit windows: their curtains swayed in a gentle breeze from the distant river; the river his family's bridge still spanned... though it was slowly crumbling. His anger began to fade because he knew Lucky was telling the truth; and it mirrored the truth he already knew but part of him still didn't want to believe. Finally he shrugged. "There probably won't be a war. I'm sure the North doesn't want one. It would tear this whole country apart."

"You told me you had some money," said Lucky.

"Yeah. ...But, what's that got to do...?"

"I think I can make you very rich. ...In useful coin of the future realm."

"...You talkin' about investments?" asked Skyler.

Cartwright passed to bottle to Skyler. "I still got that dollar you give me."

Lucky smiled. "I think I can make us all rich, Sky. If you let me do some thinkin'."

"He do be good at that," said Cartwright.

"You ain't bad at it, either," said Skyler.

"You done a lot of 'pregnatin', too."

"Pray it don't get us a shotgun wedding."

Cartwright smiled. "All for one, an' one for all."

"Which also applies to shotguns," said Skyler. "Not to mention lynchings and hangings, usually preceded by unpleasant parties."

Lucky snubbed out his cigar in Skyler's spotless chamber pot... tended and cleaned by a maid, of course. "Speakin' of money matters, your accounts aren't in very good shape, Sky. You been spending too much on luxuries like peacocks, pianos, and fancy-ass clothes; includin' clothes for your house slaves so dreary little people won't talk. But you got leaky roofs in the Quarters for the people who make all your money."

"You been snoopin'!" cried Skyler.

"Let's say I been delving for truth, which is required for productive thinkin' no matter what the subject."

Skyler shrugged. "We could use some help with that money stuff. Father was going to hire someone, but I can convince him to give you a try. ...I trust your intentions are noble."

"I trust your intentions are likewise."

"Now what you talkin' about?"

"In regard to my sister, Sir Knight."

Skyler glanced to the windows again, which overlooked the huge front lawn. "'Course they are."

Chapter Twenty-Nine

"Oh, Skyler you look so noble in white!"

His mother pinched Skyler's chubby cheeks, then swept back a pace to inspect him. "It offsets your color quite well."

"He has improved his color," said Lucky, who stood nearby with Cartwright. Both wore only trousers appropriate to the bayou theme, but Skyler was dressed in a snowy-white suit with a ruffled white shirt and a black western tie, and scowled at himself in the sewing room mirror. "I'd have to have as much color as you to make a dent in all this white!"

Cartwright grinned. "Now y'all be a white knight, suh."

Skyler's mother giggled. "Carter is so clever!"

"So I've noticed," growled Skyler.

His mother drew a pendant watch from somewhere amongst her profusion of ruffles. "Our guests will be arriving soon. Daphilla's mother sent a note... Daphilla is *so* delighted to be seeing you again."

"She won't see very much of me bedazzled by all this white," said Skyler, glaring at Cartwright and Lucky, who'd folded their arms like chicken wings. "Though I doubt she ever has."

Skyler's mother adjusted his tie. "This will be such a marvelous party! Lucrezia is such a wonderful cook! The guests won't believe it's just common food!"

"Probably 'cause they never had any." Skyler tugged his tie loose. "And it's Lucinda, mother. Lucrezia Borgia poisoned people."

"That certainly hasn't been the case here. Nothing has been the least disagreeable. ...You know I don't like to discuss business matters, but I can't believe you bought that girl for less than an astronomical sum. Or why in the world Seth Franklin would sell her." She turned to Lucky. "And along with such an intelligent boy! Your father said he's been so useful balancing those dreadful books." She gave Lucky's pendulous cheeks a pinch. "And to think he's only a slave!"

"Especially to think," said Skyler.

"Of course it's naughty that he can read, but that's our little secret."

"A rather large one, I'd call it," said Skyler.

"Oh," said his mother. "I don't wish to sully our festive mood, but I must insist that you discipline Robert for the feather incident. It's been almost a week, and they do forget."

"You mean now?" asked Skyler.

"I think it would be a proper time. He and his brother... er... Randolf..."

"Romulus and Remus, mother."

"I wanted them at the party along with the little fan boys... not serving, of course, but to shoo away insects. And for decoration appropriate to the theme. But I fear that unless Rupert is punished, he might think of taking liberties." Skyler's mother swept to the door. "Please bring him in."

The door opened, revealing Remus in only trousers. Jupiter stood behind him looking properly stern, and guided him in with a hand on his shoulder until he was standing head down before Skyler. Skyler's mother crossed her arms. "Well...?"

"You been very naughty," said Skyler.

"Yes, suh," said Remus, not looking up.

Skyler's mother frowned a bit. "I'm sure he's aware of that."

Skyler saw a strip of belt leather draped on a nearby chair. He took it and snapped it like a whip. "Turn around, boy."

Remus obediently offered his back, and Skyler drew back his arm. "Do you wish to see this, mother?"

"Heavens no! I'll wait outside."

Skyler waited until the door closed, then said loudly, "I 'spect you know what's comin', Remus?"

"Yes, massa."

Skyler swung the leather... cracking it against the chair.

"Ow!" yelled Remus.

"Louder," said Skyler, lashing the helpless chair again.

"OW!"

"How many should I give him, Cartwright?"

"I make it three for feather yankin'."

Skyler tortured the chair once more.

"OW!" yelled Remus. "I sorry, massa! I never yank no feathers again!"

"Make some tears," said Lucky.

"But he ain't got no stripes," said Cartwright.

"Mother won't look," said Skyler. He patted Remus' shoulder. "Tell me next time if you get pecked an' I'll shoot the God-dammed thing. ...An' be careful snitchin' food tonight."

"Sho', Sky."

Skyler turned to Jupiter. "Take this feather-yanker away."

Remus left the room sobbing, Jupiter following close behind to hide any glimpse of his back.

Skyler's mother peeped in. "That was excessive, don't you think? After all it was only a feather and I did need one for my hat."

Skyler glanced at Cartwright and Lucky, who stood with heads properly down. "I don't want my boys gettin' ideas."

Chapter Thirty

"**O**h, Skyler you look so noble in white!"

"*Déjà vu,*" said Skyler, taking a sip from his glass of beer, though he really wanted to gulp it down and fortify himself with another... his fifth or sixth at least. "But I haven't been feeling noble of late."

"Why ever not?" asked Daphilla, who, as far as Skyler could tell, had been sipping from the same glass of French wine for most of what he considered to be a very dreary evening... except for the meteoric food.

Daphilla was also thirteen, and had grown a bit with the passing year... at least her bosom seemed bigger in the bodice of her gown. But, so was Skyler's beneath his shirt: in fact, he thought, his might have grown more, and he knew for a fact his weren't enhanced.

Daphilla waved a delicate hand that held a silken fan, to indicate the house and grounds. "But you're going to inherit all this."

Skyler took a gulp of beer and politely muffed a burp. "As your parents are well aware."

"Of course they are," Daphilla said with a cultivated titter. "My family's plantation *is* rather large, though not as grand as yours, of course, so it's natural we should be good friends." Daphilla smiled coquettishly... which looked like a baby with gas. "Until we're both a bit older, and perhaps our relationship will flower."

"Like wreaths at a funeral," suggested Skyler.

"Oh, Skyler, how romantic! Like Romeo and Juliet eternally together."

"And both quite dead," said Skyler, draining his glass in a second

161

gulp. Cartwright offered another, and Lucky lumbered forward to straighten Skyler's tie.

Daphilla looked vexed. "Your boys are certainly attentive, we haven't been alone all evening."

Skyler smiled. "They're acutely perceptive to all my needs."

"Cartwright *is* a handsome buck and does appear to serve you well, but the... large one doesn't seem very useful."

"Oh, he's full of surprises," said Skyler.

The "bayou party" was out on the lawn in the steamy warmth of the night. Tables and chairs had been set up between the house's portico and the grassy shore of the pond. Lanterns were strung overhead on ropes, and the moon, though waning, was silvery bright. The house servants all wore appropriate dress; the males in plain canvas trousers, the kind issued to field slaves, and the women in simple dresses, though newly-made and spotless. There were also a dozen sleepy kids added for decoration, as well as keeping insects from annoying the guests. Cartwright and Lucky had stayed with Skyler, Cartwright bringing food and beer, which Lucky mostly ate and drank.

Supper had been a smashing success, the guests all praising the wonderful food -- chicken gumbo, crawfish pie, cajun sausage, "dirty rice," plump red beans, and breaded catfish -- amazed that "common folk" ate so well. Skyler's mother had brought out Lucinda for a round of polite applause. Skyler had met Lucinda's eyes, she up beneath the portico lamp, while he sat listening to Daphilla... though hearing little and caring less. Lucinda seemed to be having fun, though only he could see that.

Angel was also a decoration, charmingly clad in a new slave dress. After introducing her to Cartwright the first night back at Diligence, Skyler had asked she be moved to the house, though starting in the scullery, the only place available. Although still awkwardly shy, Cartwright had been meeting her -- tactfully arranged by Skyler -- and had made the most of her presence tonight, the only time he'd left Skyler's side, until the dessert of pie was served and the decorations sent away; most of whom would go to bed with bellies full of Lucinda's food... though Angel would be up for hours washing all the dishes.

Then the party had divided, the ladies flocking for lady-chat around the lantern-lit sitting house, while the men sipped brandy and smoked cigars. Skyler had joined them for a while because his father wished it, and the talk was mostly of recent news; of Abolitionists in the North, including the views of Abraham Lincoln who might be elected President, and the need for the South to prepare for war.

Skyler had found himself amazed that "Honor" seemed of more concern than everything Lucky had told him: no mention was made of factories – or rather the obvious lack of them -- or needing resources to fight a war. These self-styled educated men seemed to think nobility was mightier than iron and steel. While Cartwright and Lucky weren't actually there, both approached him frequently to ask if he wanted anything, and he knew they were getting an earful. Finally, he'd asked a few logical questions, sounding a bit like Lucky, which only produced a frown from his father and patronizing smiles from the others.

There was also talk about dealing with slaves, who would surely be hearing and spreading rumors; and how to guard against agitators... perhaps, until the South gathered an army, a local militia should be formed to patrol for possible runaways and question strangers passing through. The bridge would be a logical place to set up an inspection post.

Skyler wasn't sure what to feel... anger, concern, or amusement. Nor if he was cowardly, wise, or simply realistic for thinking he'd rather be somewhere else if this seemingly senseless war ever started. Then his mother had signaled that Daphilla should have his attention.

Fortunately, the party was ending. Carriages and coaches were being driven around from the stable and guests were getting aboard. Just as happily for Skyler, Lucky and Cartwright stayed with him -- to Daphilla's obvious dismay -- as he strolled with her around the pond and feigned attention to her chatter while pondering what the future might bring and what he might have to do with it.

Lucky's puffing distracted Daphilla. And of course he was sweating profusely having to perambulate, which wasn't unpleasant to

Skyler's nose compared to Daphilla's saccharine perfume, which made him think of a French Quarter "house." He slowed his pace a bit so Lucky wouldn't be left behind, and finally stopped beneath a tree to spare him further exertion.

Daphilla now looked desperate... no doubt her mother had made a list of all the proper things to say, which she hadn't managed to exhaust at dinner. She fluttered the fan in front of her face, probably because of Lucky. "Of course you'll be visiting us very soon?"

"No doubt our mothers will arrange it."

"You won't need *them*," said Daphilla, frowning at Lucky and Cartwright. "Our house has more than enough servants."

"I'm sure of that," said Skyler.

"Of course... if we *were* to become engaged... I would have to insist you have better boys. Cartwright, though I do grant handsome for a negro boy, is rather too rough for the house, and I can't understand what you see in the... large one."

"I'm also sure of that," said Skyler.

Daphilla glanced across the pond, where her parents waited beside their coach. "You *must* give me a parting kiss." She tittered. "On the cheek, of course."

"Of course," said Skyler, ignoring Cartwright, who'd stuck a finger down his throat, crossed his eyes and put out his tongue.

Suddenly, there was screech in the tree. Daphilla produced a similar sound, and there was a plop as something white and very vile fell upon her golden head.

"Horrid!" she screamed, dancing around and plucking her hair. Then she grabbed up her skirts and ran.

Skyler watched the fleeing girl as she rounded the pond like a turkey on fire, shrieking HORRID at the top of her lungs while other peacocks screamed in the trees.

Cartwright observed, "Look like she still got chicken feet, Sky."

"Yeah, I noticed that."

Chapter Thirty-One

L ucinda smiled in the silver moonlight. "So, this is the real
Knight's Crossing."

"One might call it the first," said Skyler. "It was here a before
the town, and the reason there is a town."

The four friends sat on the mighty horse, who probably hardly
noticed their weight; Skyler with Lucinda behind him, her arms
around his waist, and Angel held by Cartwright.

Two hours had passed since the party, where Skyler had left
Cartwright and Lucky convulsed with laughter behind the tree and,
trying to keep his own contained, had hurried around the pond to
apologize for the "distressing event" to an hysterical Daphilla, who
by then was surrounded by servants cooing at her like dutiful doves
while diligently cleaning the mess from her hair.

Her parents were proper, of course: "a very unfortunate accident,
but which would leave no lasting stain, they hoped, upon future
relations." Daphilla, still crying and rather bedraggled from vigorous
cleansing by many black hands, was finally assisted into the coach
and wailed to her mother as it rolled off, "I don't think he likes me!"

The other guests had bid goodnight, all congratulating Skyler as
if he'd returned from an arduous quest with a dragon's head impaled
on a pike, and servants were clearing the tables while eating and
drinking as much as they could.

Lucky and Cartwright returned to his side, Lucky taking possession of one of the surviving pies, and they had gone up to Skyler's
room to put the pie to the proper use for which most pies were
created, after which Lucky had gone to bed. By then it was nearing

midnight, but neither Skyler nor Cartwright were tired. Reverting to their buckskin -- at least to their trousers of same – they'd passed through the silent and now darkened house to the little lamp-lit scullery where Lucinda and Angel were doing the dishes and helped them finish the job.

What happened next seemed natural; Skyler taking his friends to the stable, where Billy slept on a pile of hay. The gentle horse was willing, by now accustomed to what, to him, were easy and maybe interesting tasks; and Skyler, Lucinda, Cartwright and Angel had ridden off to the bridge.

Skyler studied the structure now in the gentle glow of the moon; built of massive timbers, now covered with moss and shrouded in vines, it spanned the river in three great leaps bedded on piers of quarried stone that slaves had hauled for many miles through hellish summer bayou heat and icy winter rain.

"It still looks strong, but the wood is rotten. An' there's no more trees that size around here, so there's no way to rebuild it. Not the way it was, anyhow."

"I'd like to cross it," said Lucinda. "It's a beautiful night for a walk."

"With beautiful friends," said Cartwright, and Angel smiled at him.

Skyler and Cartwright slid off the horse and helped the girls to the ground. Then, Skyler taking Lucinda's hand, Cartwright taking Angel's, they started across the bridge. The river flowed quietly beneath them, glistening under the moon; bullfrogs boomed on the reedy banks, and fireflies danced among the vines that draped the mossy timbers. Cartwright laughed as heavy clops trembled the planks behind them. "Our horse like moonlight walkin', too."

"What's his name?" asked Lucinda.

"He doesn't have one," said Skyler. "Being only a work beast."

"He seems much more than that." Lucinda smiled. "How about Hengroen?"

Skyler laughed. "King Arthur's horse?"

"One of them, anyway. He had two."

Skyler nodded. "A stallion, Hengroen, and a mare, Llamrei.

...Rocinante might be more appropriate."

Lucinda pressed his hand. "You haven't been tilting at windmills, Sir Knight, and your steed deserves a noble name."

"She's right, Sky," said Cartwright, and indicated Skyler's knife. "May I?"

"...Oh. Of course."

Cartwright drew the big blade, gleaming in the moonlight, and touched its flat to the horse's shoulder. "I dub thee Hengroen."

Skyler bowed to the gigantic horse. "May I prove worthy of you."

They continued on and were halfway across when Hengroen suddenly stopped. His ears flicked erect, and he swung his great head to look back. Cartwright whispered, "Just like he done a'fore we found Andrew."

Skyler looked back where the road disappeared into shadows of trees like the mouth of a railroad tunnel. "We'd have heard another horse by now, or a wagon or coach."

Cartwright pointed. "Somebody in them bushes, Sky!"

Lucinda whispered, "Why would someone be hiding from us?"

Skyler wondered if one of the night watch might have followed them. Of course he could order him to leave, though the man would probably tell his father. ...But, what had he done that was wrong?

Cartwright cried, "There he go, Sky!"

"Cartwright! No!" yelled Skyler, as Cartwright bolted off in pursuit.

"Stay here with the horse!" Skyler called to the girls as he dashed, puffing, after Cartwright. The night watch wouldn't have run away.

A shadow had burst from the bushes like a rabbit flushed in a hunt. Skyler was no match for Cartwright's speed, and still hadn't reached the end of the bridge, but saw a figure run back up the road. It was only a shadow in shadows, though it moved as if possibly wounded or hurt. Cartwright caught up in a second, diving for the figure's legs, and both thudded down in the dirt. There were traded punches and curses, then Skyler reached them and joined the fray. It was too dark to see who it was, but it didn't feel like a full-grown man, although possessed of powerful muscles and an obvious desperation to use them. Skyler finally got hold of an arm. Then he grabbed the other arm and pinned them behind a sturdy back. Cartwright seized the kicking bare feet, and they wrestled a struggling black boy into a patch of silver moonlight.

Terrified eyes stared up at Skyler. Then the boy, maybe fifteen, went limp and started to plead.

"I didn't know you was white, suh! I sorry, suh! I sorry!"

Cartwright took over from Skyler and hauled the boy to his feet, still pinning his arms behind his back.

"Be quiet!" panted Skyler, yanking up his slipping trousers. He glanced at the bridge as the girls came running, Hengroen clopping behind. Then he studied the half-naked boy; chest like paving stones heaving for breath, trousers in rags muddied up to the knees, and dirty and dripping sweat from the fight. "Who you belong to?" he demanded. "And don't you lie to me!"

The boy hesitated a moment, staring now at the girls, then at the enormous horse. Tears began to roll down his cheeks, making shiny rivulets in mud. "Massa Crawford at Cypress, suh."

Skyler scowled. "Cypress is ten miles away. What are you doing here on your own in the middle of the night?"

"...Massa Crawford need the doctor."

Skyler drew back his hand for a slap, but then gripped the boy's shoulders and looked in his eyes. "I warned you not to lie to me. If Crawford needed the doctor he would have sent someone on a horse." He paused to study the boy again. "You ain't been travelin' the roads, not with all that mud to your knees, your trousers all ripped and those leaves in your hair. You been tryin' to get though the bayou... till you got stopped by the river and came here to cross the bridge."

Cartwright shook the boy, though the boy was a full head taller and probably twice as strong. "Ain't no use in lyin'," he warned. "'Specially when you ignorant an' don't even know what you lyin' about."

The boy began to cry again, and dropped his chin to his chest. "...I... run away."

Angel's eyes flew wide -- to her this would be the ultimate sin, like Lucifer defying God -- but Lucinda stepped to Skyler's side and gently lifted the big boy's chin.

"Where were you going?" She turned to Skyler. "You said this road goes to New Orleans?"

"It does... which doesn't make sense." Skyler eyed the boy. "Can't you even tell north from south on a moonlit night with stars in the sky?"

The boy had been looking at Lucinda, curious despite himself why she would be out with a white boy at night. And what of the other two slaves? Then something like hope lit his eyes. "Y'all work on the railroad?"

Skyler scowled again. "What do you know about that?"

"...Nothin', suh." The glow of hope died and the boy dropped his head.

Skyler lifted his jaw. "Maybe I'll forget that. But why were you going south?"

"...They say they's ships go to islands where black folks all be free."

"Who told you that?"

"'Spect it only slave-talk, suh."

"Don't...!" Skyler began, but Lucinda moved closer to the boy and began plucking leaves from his hair.

"Let him go, Cartwright," she said. "He's too worn out for any more fighting."

"Been two days gone," said the boy, as Cartwright freed his arms. "Nothin' to eat but turtles an' frogs, an' nothin' to drink but bayou water."

"Don't sound like you did much plannin'," said Skyler. "For your future freedom. ...Or did you think milk an' honey were gonna rain on you from the sky?"

"Please don't send me back, suh!"

Skyler frowned. "Crawford doesn't mistreat his slaves." He turned the boy around and brushed the sweaty dirt from his back. "Not a scar on you 'cept brambles an' such. What put it into your head to run?"

"I wanna be free."

Skyler sighed. "If wishes were horses. ...Freedom ain't all you think it might be if you don't know how to take care of yourself."

"...Was hopin' I could learn, suh."

"You haven't made a very good start."

Cartwright said, "He gonna be punished bad, Sky, even his massa be kind."

Skyler sighed again. "Tell me somethin' I don't know."

"You could kill him, Sky."

Angel gasped.

"Please, suh, no!" cried the boy.

"*Look* at him, Cartwright," said Skyler, inspecting the boy like his father would. "Good sound teeth, big strong muscles. And except for goin' two days without food... 'cause he wasn't smart enough to store some away before he ran... does he look like he hasn't been well fed, wormed, and decently cared for?"

Skyler turned to Lucinda, who'd taken Angel's hand. "This isn't the same as what happened with Andrew. I can't just say I killed him; I'd have to return his body to Crawford. ...And I can't afford to buy a big strong buck like him."

"Can't you just let him go?" asked Lucinda, and Angel looked astonished.

Again Skyler sighed. "It's over a hundred miles to 'Orleans. He'd have to try to steal food... something he obviously isn't good at 'cause he's never had to... and someone *would* probably kill him. And most other slaves would be scared to help him... assuming he could get close to any past their Quarters watch." He faced the boy again. "You didn't think of that either, did you? How *alone* you are when you're free."

Skyler turned back to his friends. "Crawford has surely reported him gone and telegraphed his description to every town in fifty miles. And there are probably posters, so bounty-hunters are lookin' for him... maybe even the *thing* that got Andrew. Only reason he got this far is they probably think he headed north... never heard talk of runaway slaves gettin' on ships and sailin' to islands."

Lucinda looked thoughtful. "Wouldn't that be logical since the British abolished slavery on their Caribbean islands?"

Skyler shrugged. "If there's an underground railroad, maybe

there's 'underwater ships,' but he'd never get to one on his own. The land south of here is mostly swamp, so he'd have to stay on the road. He doesn't have any papers, and he *looks* like a runaway." He turned again to the boy. "What's your name? ...And we already know you ain't good at lyin'."

"Dante, suh."

"That's certainly appropriate for the hell you've put yourself in."

Lucinda said, "Let him go to Content."

"...Huh?"

Cartwright touched Skyler's shoulder. "Nobody look for him there, Sky."

"...Well..." said Skyler. "Reckon you're right... slaves don't run away to more slavery. ...But, it's hanging a sword over Franklin's head. Dante belongs to Crawford, so that would make it stealing."

"Franklin will help him," said Lucinda.

Skyler flicked his eyes to Angel. "Does that mean what I think it does?"

Lucinda smiled. "I don't know what you think it means, but I *know* you know what's right."

Skyler looked up at the stars. He wondered if God was watching, and why He wasn't helping if Dante deserved to be free. But what did he expect... an angel with a flaming sword commanding him to help this boy?

"I doubt he could make it to Franklin's. He's obviously exhausted. Besides, he'd have to go through town and someone would probably see him... be dawn by the time he got that far."

Cartwright said, "We could take him back to Diligence, Sky, an' keep him in our room. Clean him up an' feed him. We go to Content tomorrow night... take a wagon an' hide him in back."

Skyler sighed once more. "That sounds just like what I think it is, and whether it is or not." He glanced at the sky again. "Shouldn't be hard to sneak him in... everyone sleepin' off the party. And Lucky's been working on the books and getting' food brought up to his room, so Dante could stay with him all day. ...But we're not givin' Angel a choice about gettin' mixed up in something that could get all of us hung."

171

Angel's eyes widened. "Even you, suh?"

"*Especially* me," said Skyler, "for reasons you may not understand."

"...I want to help," said Angel.

Skyler looked at Cartwright again. "This is what comes from breeding ideas."

Cartwright smiled. "Seem like we bred us some good ones, Sky."

Chapter Thirty-Two

kyler and Lucinda kissed in the doorway of her little room.
Angel had returned to the Quarters, and Cartwright had taken
Dante upstairs, along with a heaping platter of food. A clock
somewhere had just chimed two, but now the huge house was silent
again.

Lucinda and Skyler parted at last, and Skyler glanced into the
room, where a candle glowed on a battered old dresser, its light revealing a small rope bed neatly made with Lucinda's own quilt. "You
deserve a castle, Milady."

Lucinda smiled. "A simple cottage would do quite well, with a bit
of garden, sir."

"Somewhere there's a place like that. And we'll find it in our
travels." Skyler bowed. "Goodnight, Milady, an' pleasant dreams."

He crossed the shadowy kitchen and opened the door to the
dining room. Moonlight shone in through the windows... then he
froze, seeing his mother in nightgown and cap sitting in one of the
chairs. Had she seen Dante with Cartwright? But she would have
thought Dante was theirs... possibly one of the "bayou boys" still in
party costume. Then she spoke, and Skyler knew what she had seen.

"That would have been all I needed, son; a simple cottage, a bit
of garden... and your father as he was at your age before he sur-
rendered to this place."

Skyler could see in her eyes that she loved him; not that he'd
ever doubted it, but he'd always only assumed she did, as if it was a
mother's duty instead of a woman's choice. But, seeing wasn't neces-
sary because his heart could feel her love, the way he felt Lucinda's

love, something as soft as summer rain but also as strong as oak. "How long have you known?" he asked.

His mother smiled. "That you were in love with someone? Since the first day you came home. And of course I knew it wasn't Daphilla... to think you could ever be happy with her!" Then her face saddened. "But, this love between you and Lucinda is just not possible, son."

"We'll find a place where it's right."

His mother sighed. "Of course, it's right. But, what is right is not always possible." She held out her hands to Skyler, and took his when he came over. "This world is not ruled by what is right; this world is ruled by hate and greed. By lies, deception, and most of all fear."

"I'm not afraid," said Skyler. "Though I think I'm smart enough to know when to battle and when to retreat."

His mother nodded. "Bravery is like a sword, but wisdom is knowing when to draw it. And here your foes are legion. ...You know I am not from this place?"

"Of course," said Skyler. "You're from Providence, in Rhode Island. Father met you there."

"Then you know I have had to learn much here, and accept many things that are wrong to my heart. ...At least to act as if I accept them." His mother sighed again. "Perhaps I have acted so well and so long that at times I forget I am acting." She turned to a moonlit window. "Perhaps someday the world will learn how to love what is right, but I know I will never see that day. Nor, I fear, will you."

"There must be *some* good place," said Skyler. "Perhaps very small and far away, undiscovered, or maybe forgotten."

Again his mother's smile was sad. "You *are* a noble young knight. The son that most mothers long for, yet fear."

"Fear?" asked Skyler.

"Because we know we will lose you. This world does not love noble young knights, because by your right you reveal its wrongs."

Skyler pressed his mother's hands. "I have no wish to cause you pain."

"I know that, son, but you will. And as a mother I accept it.

Perhaps it is good that you have a wildness, something I've always felt in you. A strength, perhaps, from a time long ago." Her eyes met Skyler's again, loving yet sad, gentle yet strong, and she gestured to indicate the house. "You would give up all this for the right of your love?"

"My 'lands and title?'" said Skyler. "Land that was stolen from native people? A 'castle' built by the labor of slaves? 'Nobility' I never earned? ...Yes, our family worked, long ago. We created things with our own hands. And no doubt suffered hardship." He pointed out toward the Quarters. "But we never suffered a fraction of theirs... suffering *we* forced on them. We have prospered but they still suffer. We have risen by holding them down, and some day that wrong will have to be paid for. I'm thirteen years in debt already, forging chains I may have to drag like Marley's ghost forever. But maybe it's not too late to break them. And maybe in some, if only small way, I can begin to make amends."

Again his mother sighed. "You are indeed a noble young knight and I will lose you to your quest." She kissed Skyler's cheek. "Of course, your father does not know, though that is only a matter of time; and of course he could never permit such a love... even by calling it something else, as a lesser man might do. Perhaps he would send you abroad, 'until you came to your senses.' Yet, somewhere inside it would hurt him, for in his heart... In a place in his heart I saw long ago, he would know you are right."

Then she gripped Skyler's shoulders. "But, whatever it is you believe you must do, you must do it before the war begins or there may be no escape."

"You know there will be war?" asked Skyler.

"Of course I know there will be a war. Men, as yet, must have them because they cannot live in peace with their hearts, or suffer the peace of those who can."

Chapter Thirty-Three

"**Y**ou're the Master now, son. Remember, you have every right under God."

Skyler stood on mansion's vast porch, watching his father climb onto his horse. Months of Lucinda's delicious cooking had given the man a prosperous figure, but that didn't hinder his grace in the saddle; and he looked noble in a gray uniform. He'd been given the rank of colonel, although he knew nothing of war except what he'd read in books, and was leaving to take command of his troops.

Skyler had added a few pounds himself, outgrowing his last pair of buckskin trousers and passing them on to Cartwright. He'd also gotten dramatically tan; and the guests at his mother's frequent parties joked that he looked like an Indian boy... though they probably thought something else.

"Are you sure what you're doing is right?" he asked, as his father donned his riding gloves. "You could have stayed out of this trouble. Besides, they still haven't declared a war."

"We have to defend our way of life." The man waved a hand to encompass the scene. "Our family settled this once wild land and made it produce like a garden. We created this greatness."

Skyler looked around at the huge white house and the lush emerald lawn with its sparkling pond being tended by Romulus and Remus, while other youths raked the graveled drive and trimmed the stately ranks of hedges. Many more slaves were out in the fields, while others worked inside the house, as well as the stables and blacksmith shop. It was hard to keep track of how many there were;

there had been several births in the last few months. Still, there were over a hundred -- men, women, boys and girls -- and Skyler was now their master. He could starve them, whip them, order them hung, and answer to no one for doing it. He could sell babies away from their mothers, children away from their parents, and husbands away from their wives. He could brand them if he wanted to, and use them any way he chose.

His father smiled. "Don't worry, son. Jupiter's here to advise you, and we're making a handsome profit now with Lucky in charge of the books. You surely did well to buy that boy, even with all his impudence. And the war won't last but a month or so, even if it is declared."

Skyler frowned. "Then why did mother go to Providence?"

"She hasn't seen her sister in years, and of course her parents are getting on." Skyler's father glanced at the butler, who stood in the doorway, and lowered his voice:

"I thought it best she not be here in case there is some unpleasantness. But, I'll likely be home very soon, and everything will be as it was." He gave his son a jaunty salute, then flicked the reins and rode away.

Jacob stood waiting to close the doors. "I'm sho' everythin' be fine, Masta Knight. Just like your wise father say."

"I'm sure it will," said Skyler. But he only said that to reassure Jacob. It wouldn't do to seem upset or else the slaves would talk. It was fortunate they couldn't read because the news was far from good: the North seemed determined to end slavery... though the South called it "Southern Independence." Lucky predicted a long, brutal war, one in which the South would lose and all its greatness pass away... "greatness" built on the backs of slaves: a garden watered by blood, sweat and tears.

Lucky had put all of Skyler's money into northern industries, and Skyler was rich and growing richer. Telegrams seemed to arrive every day with news of more money he'd made as the North prepared to fight this war and profits soared in factories.

Lucky was growing ever fatter, and had asked for a desk in his room. He also had his meals brought up, and spent many hours with paperwork, managing the plantation's affairs as well as Skyler's investments. Cartwright rode almost daily to town to pick up or send telegrams, and Lucky was making the most of this time because there wouldn't be telegraph service, and mail would cease from the northern states when war was finally declared. The plantation's profits had also fattened, and yet more money was spent on its slaves: they were better fed and clothed these days, and the Quarters cabins all boasted new roofs against the coming winter.

"Jacob?" asked Skyler. "Do you ever think about being free?"

The butler looked astonished. "Lord no, Masta Knight! I wouldn't have such an idea in my head!"

"Well," said Skyler. "You could still work here, but you'd get paid. And you could quit if you wanted to."

"But I don't know nothin' 'bout freedom, suh! An' where would I go if I... quit? Lord forbid!" Jacob lowered his voice as the pair of fan boys came running past waving wooden swords. "I hate them Abolitionists, suh! Colored folks ain't meant to be free! We don't know how to take care of ourselves."

"That's a bad idea," said Skyler. "And it's one we put in your heads."

Jacob wrung his hands. "Please, Masta Knight, don't say any more! I been in your house all my life, suh, just like my daddy a'fore me, an' I don't want nothin' to change!"

"A lot of people are scared of change, even when it's right," said Skyler.

Jacob politely closed his face. "Will there be anythin' else, suh?"

"No, thank you." Skyler entered the house and ran up the stairs. He swam almost daily with Cartwright; and Lucky often came along... in the back of a wagon. Skyler took many long walks with Lucinda to pretty and secluded places -- the bridge, the bayou, a pond in the woods -- where they talked while she painted her pictures, and carried his chubbiness easily. He wasn't even breathing hard when he reached his room.

Cartwright was lounging on Skyler's bed in only his buckskin trousers. He hadn't gained much noticeable weight, unless one counted muscles. Angel was sitting beside him, plumper and cuter than ever. They were looking at pictures in what might have been a magazine, though Cartwright could now read a little and was learning more every day thanks to Lucky's tutoring.

Cartwright looked up as Skyler came in. "You couldn't change your daddy's mind?"

Skyler shook his head. "I did my best, but it wouldn't be 'honorable' to refuse his commission... even though, realistically, he could be of more help to the 'Noble Cause' by staying here and raising food. I just hope he's right an' there isn't a war. Or, if there is, it won't last long."

Then he smiled. "But, since I'm the master now, you'll have your freedom papers today... if Lucky ain't sleepin' as usual."

"I'm wide awake," called Lucky from the adjoining room. "And those papers were finished an hour ago, so get in here and sign 'em."

Skyler went into Lucky's room. The enormous boy lay on his bed looking rather majestic in a very large pair of buckskin trousers. He was eating a piece of pecan pie; and Skyler recalled their first night together.

"There *will* be a war," said Lucky, around a mouthful of pie. "Thanks to a lot of bad ideas. And it will go on for years. But, I hope your daddy will be all right."

"Thanks," said Skyler. "I know you do."

He looked out the windows, seeing the lawn and the slaves at work... a typical day at Diligence. Peacocks strutted here and there, and the pond lay as still as a mirror. Then he went to the desk and picked up a pen. Dipping it into a bottle of ink, he signed the papers for Angel and Cartwright, creating a pair of free human beings, then took them in to Cartwright.

"You can leave whenever you want. Take a train North before they stop runnin'. And you have some back pay comin'... thirteen years by my calculations."

Cartwright and Angel looked surprised. "But, we don't want to leave you," said Cartwright. "An' not 'cause we can't take care of ourselves." He held out what he'd been reading; a pamphlet with pictures of ships for sale. "Look at this sixty-foot steam schooner,

Sky. You could go anywhere in the world on her, an' I can run the engine."

Skyler regarded the picture of a two-masted schooner with a tall smokestack. "But, I don't know anything about the sea, or how to sail somethin' like that."

"Ain't no reason you couldn't learn, it just another new idea; an' it only take a few people to sail her... friends who want to see the world."

Lucky waddled in. "Friends including Danny an' me. Been doing some reading about navigation, so I can plot your course."

"You seem very good at that," said Skyler. "...Well, it's somethin' to think about." He turned to Cartwright and Angel. "But for now I think you should leave. Whatever is coming ain't gonna be good."

Angel smiled. "Bein' your friend is good, Sky."

"An' that's already here," said Cartwright.

"But, friends protect each other," said Skyler. "And staying here could be dangerous." He faced Lucky again. "I want papers for Jupiter and his missus. He's got back pay comin', too... seventy years of it. That ought to buy 'em a cottage somewhere."

"Already drawn up," said Lucky.

"And papers for you and Lucinda?"

"At Content... where they always were... and Frankin is sending 'em over today."

"...Huh?" said Skyler. "You already have freedom papers?"

Lucky laughed. "That's why Franklin 'traded' us for Andrew; you can't buy free human beings."

"...I don't understand," said Skyler.

"It's our System, Sky. ...Which is why you could never figure it out. There ain't no slaves at Content, and haven't been for years. The people are there 'cause they want to be."

"...You mean they could leave whenever they want?"

Lucky's face saddened a little. "Where would they go? Back to Africa, a place they know almost nothing about? And the North and West ain't all free, either; there's still lots of people who hate us. At Content they have a peaceful village. And their kids can have a child-hood instead of workin' all day. Franklin only acts like the master so whitefolks don't ask questions; but everyone shares in Content's profits. And everyone can read. Franklin teaches the kids while he fishes."

Skyler nodded slowly. "I should have suspected something like that, but it would have seemed impossible."

"Which is why you didn't," said Lucky. "Nor all the other masters 'round here. Black and white people living as equals and working together is something they can't, or don't want to, believe."

Skyler turned to Cartwright. "'Spose you knew all the time?"

"Not at first," said Cartwright. "Lucky told me some things at the station first day I come to Knight's Crossin'. 'Course, I didn't believe him then. Thought he was givin' me bad ideas so I'd run away to Content."

"You could have," said Skyler. "No one would have known. You could have disappeared like Dante."

"I'm glad I didn't, 'cause I'd never met you."

Skyler went to Cartwright and hugged him. "And I would have never met you."

"Hey," said Lucky. "What about me?"

Skyler laughed and hugged the huge boy. "All for one and one for all." Then he cocked his head. "But, why would you and Lucinda come here and let yourselves be treated like slaves?"

Lucky glanced at his comfortable room. "It ain't been bad being your 'slave,' and you're better at being a friend than a master. And my sister loves you... though sometimes I still can't figure out why. But you needed some education before you were worthy of her. ...Not to mention worthy of me."

"But, what's gonna happen if there's a war?"

"Change will happen," said Lucky. "And it won't all be for good." He pointed out the window. "All this will pass away, Sky. And all the people who thought it was right, who profited from and were privileged by it, will hate us for generations to come. There's something evil seeps into the earth in places where men have enslaved other men. For a long time after the war is over this land is gonna be poisoned with hate by people licking their festering wounds and still believing their wrong was right. That's why you're gonna travel, Sky.

You don't belong in a place full of hate."

"Castles and pyramids," said Lucinda coming in from the hall. She laughed. "And maybe Bohemia, too. But we still have time for lunch."

Skyler bowed and kissed her hand. Lucky was right as usual, he *had* been thinking of travel... and why not on their own little ship? They were all young; they could learn new things. Then he looked out the window. "There's something you don't see every day!"

Lucinda came to his side, followed by Cartwright, Angel and Lucky.

An enormous horse had come up the drive, so fat it looked like a huge water barrel with a head at one end and a tail at the other. "Little" Danny was at the reins, and there was a chubby young boy behind him.

"That gotta be Andrew," said Cartwright.

"He's lookin' quite prosperous now," said Skyler.

The waddling horse had reached the pond and seemed to be trying to drink it dry. Romulus and Remus were frantically trying to shoo it away.

Skyler watched the antics below, noting the hoof prints across the lawn like a pile-driver had gone on parade. "That's all right," he called to the boys. Then he took Lucinda's hand. "Don't seem like nice lawns and pretty fish ponds are gonna be very important soon. And I 'spect all the peacocks are gonna get eaten no matter how nasty they probably taste."

The huge horse finally quenched its thirst and waddled its way to the front of the house. Andrew dismounted to help Danny down; and at last they were all in the library.

"I sho' is thirsty!" puffed Danny, plopping his rolly bulk in a chair.

Andrew patted his own chubby tummy. "An' we's hungry, too."

Lucinda smiled. "Lunch will be served in fifteen minutes."

Danny searched under his blubber and extracted an envelope. "Gots a letter from Mister Franklin, 'long with Lucky an' Lucy's papers... reckon you know all about 'em by now?"

"I 'spect there's still some surprises," said Skyler.

Andrew grinned. "We brought you one. I go out an' get it."

Lucky smiled. "'Spect he'd be one of our crew, too, when we set sail to see the world."

"I'm starting to see that picture," said Skyler. "A real pretty one like Lucinda paints. But we have a lot of planning ahead."

"What's in that letter might help," said Danny.

Skyler opened the letter, scanned it quickly, then read it aloud to his friends. It began by explaining the system -- which Lucky had already done -- and ended by saying Content had been sold. Franklin and his "associates" had purchased a little Caribbean island, and all were leaving within the week to start a brand new life. Skyler and *his* associates were always welcome to join them.

Lucinda took Skyler's hand. "Maybe a place with a cottage and a bit of garden."

Skyler smiled. "To return to after our travels." Then he turned back to Lucky. "You're gonna be slaving away for awhile writin' a bunch of freedom papers for anyone here who wants to leave... though there will probably be a few who won't be able to understand that being free does not come free."

Andrew returned bearing Franklin's sword and offered it to Skyler. "He say it yours now, Sky."

Lucky lumbered forward. "I believe I have the authority, being one of the order myself."

Lucinda laughed. "Kneel, Sky."

"...Oh," said Skyler. "But, Cartwright is the worthy one."

"You've both left a few dragons bleeding," said Lucky.

Skyler took Cartwright's hand, and both boys sank to their knees. Lucky gently touched their shoulders with the flat of the gleaming blade. "Arise, sir knights," he said. "Your quest has just begun."

The End

About The Author

Jess Mowry was born in 1960 near Starkville, Mississippi. When he was only a few months old his father took him to live in Oakland, California. Mowry's father was a voracious reader who introduced his son to books at a very early age. Jess attended a public school, but despite his love of reading, dropped out at age thirteen, part way through the eighth grade and worked with his father in the scrap-iron business. In his late teens, Jess moved to Arizona to work as a truck driver and heavy equipment operator. He also lived and worked in Alaska as an engineer aboard a tugboat and as an aircraft mechanic on Douglas C-47 cargo planes, as well as at a children's refuge in Haiti.

Mowry has written twenty-five books and many short stories about black children and teens in a variety of genres, ranging from inner-city settings to the forests of Haiti, the wilds of Alaska, the Arizona desert, the Caribbean Sea, and the African veldt. While some of his novels are set in Oakland and deal with social issues, such as poverty, violence, drugs, gangs, teenage sexuality, and school drop-outs, Mowry has also written ghost tales, as well as novels featuring Voodoo and African magic, in addition to sea stories, and compiled an anthology of Victorian ghost stories.

Jess Mowry lives in Oakland, California.

THIS BOOK IS ALSO AVAILABLE IN A KINDLE EDITION

OTHER ANUBIS BOOKS

AVAILABLE ON AMAZON